ENDORSEMENTS

"Every ministry leader, board member, and development staff needs to read this novel. This book will change your heart, change your mind, and change your methods for how resources are mobilized for your ministry and God's work."

—BRIAN KLUTH
Bestselling author of *40 Day Journey
to a Generous Life* and *Experience God as Your Provider*

"The Third Conversion uniquely captures the true meaning of fundraising as a ministry to the donor as well as the significance of seeking joy in giving by the donor. Scott Rodin challenges the reader by 'sowing' in their minds, hearts, and souls, the significance of stewardship, integrity, excellence, and the Lord's rightful place in the relationship between the development professional, the organization, and the donor. I could not help but pause and deeply reflect upon the author's story-based approach to emphasizing, with a rich theological perspective, the importance of properly stewarding those relationships God has entrusted us with. A powerful book."

—JOHN CLAUSE
Former Vice President—Development, World Vision, Inc.

"Finally someone has given the Christian community a refreshing and entertaining narrative on biblical stewardship. I encourage you to put down that insipid fundraising manual and pick up Scott Rodin's *The Third Conversion*. It's a freeing, fun read for board members, CEOs, development professionals, and even donors—one that's filled with why-dos and how-tos regarding a philosophy of stewardship that can produce financial transactions as well as spiritual transformations."

—JOHN ASHMEN
President, Association of Gospel Rescue Missions

"Scott Rodin brings the joy of the ministry of stewardship for fund-raisers, those who supervise them, and the donors that make that calling possible, to life. Demonstrating his seasoned experience as a fundraising professional as well as his masterful ability to weave biblical truths and insights into meaningful real-world stories, Scott inspires, convicts, cajoles, and equips the reader to embrace a model of Christ-centered stewardship that will transform those that embrace it.... Dr. Rodin reminds us that God's stewardship work, done God's stewardship way, will result in much more than funded projects and balanced budgets—it produces freed-indeed, joy-filled stewards."

—DR. DAVID J. GYERTSON
Distinguished Professor of Leadership Formation
and Renewal, Regent University

"Scott Rodin's vivid vignettes from the life of a fictional ministry fund-raiser deftly but compassionately slipped the dagger of Scripture's two-edged sword right into my rib cage. His penetrating biblical critique calls us to *repent and be converted* when it comes to our tendency to substitute superficial sanctification of our fundraising principles and practices for radical commitment to steward ourselves and shepherd our ministry partners toward a lifestyle of richness toward God. Get ready to be uncomfortable."

—RALPH E. ENLOW JR.
President, Association for Biblical Higher Education

"We intuitively know that generating revenue for God's work is somehow different from fundraising as used in the broader non-profit context—but the difference has at times been hard to articulate. In *The Third Conversion*, Scott Rodin nails it! He brilliantly uses the genre of business fiction to explain what makes ministry fundraising different—and why it is real ministry, not just 'ministry support.'"

—GARY WILLIAMS
Founder and National Director, Christian Management Australia

"As effective as any textbook on raising support, as transforming as any verse-by-verse study of what the Bible says about raising money for ministry, this story of a fundraiser becoming a steward leader lays out the model for where raising support for ministry must go in the Christian community. Everyone in the ministry partnership—donors, workers, board members, executives—benefits from reading, reflecting on, and then implementing what they discover here."

—MARK L. VINCENT, PH.D., CSP, Senior Design Partner and CEO, Design Group International

"Read this book. It's both spiritually rich and easily readable. Rodin will warmly draw you in and guide you on a grace-filled journey of understanding the role Christian leaders must *and must not* play in the lives of people related to encouraging Christian generosity. Be open to what God may do in your life, too, because if you are, your leadership may never be the same."

—GARY HOAG
Generosity Monk

"The Third Conversion is a fun read that delivers a compelling message to all who are involved in resourcing God's Kingdom. The story models the importance of encouraging people to become rich toward God while trusting God for the provision of resources. It is a distinct message and one that will have dramatic impact on more of God's people experiencing the joy of giving."

—TODD HARPER
President, Generous Giving

"Scott Rodin has blessed his readers again with this story of Carl and Walt's journey from secular fundraising to true ministry and from bondage to freedom. *The Third Conversion* is a powerful picture of the role faith plays in fundraising—and life! May we all be the joyful, obedient, and faithful stewards God created us to be."

—BRIAN SIMMONS
President, Association of Christian Schools International

The THIRD CONVERSION

A NOVELETTE

R. SCOTT RODIN

KINGDOM LIFE PUBLISHING

BREAKING RULES

W alter Rodgers knew he was in for two very challenging days. He tried to concentrate on the road as he navigated his Prius along a crowded Interstate 5 toward downtown Seattle. The scene through his windshield was all-too familiar: rows of red taillights glowing through intermittent swipes of wipers clearing away the cold winter rain. Thankfully, the slow moving traffic gave him time to reflect on the work that awaited him.

Walt had been working at Hands of Love International (which had the fortunate acronym HOLI) for the last seventeen years. His journey there had taken him from an entry-level major gifts officer to the director of major and planned gifts, followed by a short stint as the director of strategic planning before culminating in the last seven years at his current post as the vice president for international resource development.

Walt came to the fundraising profession later in his career after having served successfully in several sales and marketing positions, mostly in the professional services industry. When he sensed a call from God to invest his skills and time in ministry-related work, it seemed a natural transition to go from sales to fundraising. The leadership at the time he joined HOLI agreed. The training seminars and workshops he attended over the next several years confirmed for him that fundraising was really no more than sales with a spin.

Walt shook his head as he thought about those early days and how hard he tried to figure out how his faith played a role in his fundraising work. He asked the question of several "experts" in the field, but no one seemed too concerned about the need to integrate the two, other than offering some general platitudes like "cover your work in prayer" and "trust God to bless your work." They were nice thoughts, but he had wondered if there wasn't something more to it, something that should set apart work done for God's glory, something that made it uniquely Christian. But, since no one seemed to be asking such questions, and his organization was content with his approach to his work, Walt simply set the issue aside as questions for another day.

The traffic opened up and Walt guided his hybrid onto the Mercer Street exit. The Space Needle loomed almost directly overhead as he entered the parking lot of the national headquarters, which was affectionately referred to as the "HOLI Lot." As he left his car and entered the main entrance of the modest office complex, he recalled how he had many times come through these doors to share news of the fruits of his work with an anxious leadership and staff.

He remembered the intense pressure of those early days when he carried his success on his own shoulders. He recalled the overwhelming weight of that burden when he brought back the bad news that a much smaller gift had been given than what was hoped for or, even worse, no gift at all. It was easy for Walt to relive those feelings of anxiety, even though they were now vestiges of an old and discarded framework for raising support at HOLI.

Walt made his way back to his office, but he didn't turn on his laptop. He wouldn't be here long. He had arrived just early enough to pray and prepare for his day. He sat behind his desk and looked quickly through the mail and memos that awaited him. He made a few quick notes, set them aside, and then closed his doors to give him the space to think and pray.

Once he had cleared his mind, he picked up the lone file lying at the center of his desk. He opened it to scan once again the resume of Carl Burns. He hoped that reviewing Carl's strong credentials would ease his anxiety over this most recent and strategic hire. Walt had one inviolable principle for hiring key major ministry partner staff: they must understand and be committed to a biblical approach to raising resources for the ministry. For Walt, that meant a focus on being used by the Holy Spirit to help their ministry supporters develop hearts that are rich toward God. Over the years, Walt had turned away many seasoned fundraising professionals because of this unequivocal standard. And now, at the point in his career where Walt knew he needed to build the team that would take over after his retirement, he had chosen to break his own rule and take the biggest gamble of his professional life.

Carl Burns had an impressive pedigree. Walt scanned down the resume page while reminding himself of Carl's outstanding preparation for this new role at HOLI. Carl had spent over ten years in various development positions for a national ministry, followed by eight years as the chief major gifts officer at St. Luke's Medical Center, a large hospital in Arizona. During his years at the hospital, he had earned every credential and attended most all fundraising seminars and workshops available. In the last five years, he had become a leading voice in the training of major gifts officers in the hospital industry. He had written successfully and was responsible for a significant increase in giving to the hospital and its foundation. Carl had explained to Walt in the final interview how deeply he missed investing his skills in Christian work and was excited about the opportunity to lead the major gifts team at HOLI.

Everything HOLI needed seemed to be there in Carl's resume—the experience, the training, and the calling. Yet in all of the time that Walt had spent with Carl in the interview process, Walt never heard Carl articulate a biblical understanding for how money was to be raised for Christian work. On two occasions, Walt came close to rejecting Carl as the final candidate, and yet something kept bringing him back to this resume. When Walt offered Carl the job, he told Carl straight out that this was the one concern he held, and he secured from Carl his full commitment to discuss this concern as they worked together toward meeting the financial goals of the organization.

Today marked the beginning point for that discussion. Carl would be at the office in twenty minutes to begin two days of calls on current and prospective new ministry supporters. Walt checked his phone to make sure there were no changes or updates in the appointments he had set. He pulled the files on the five people that he and Carl would visit and placed them in his briefcase. Then he took a deep breath, leaned forward in his chair, placed his elbows on his desk, and folded his hands to pray.

First Steps

The knock on his door brought Walt out of his prayer time before he was finished. It was Carl, who had arrived ten minutes early. Walt greeted him, and the two sat down together to discuss their game plan for the day. Carl was fifteen years younger than Walt and had an air of professionalism about him that Walt knew would play well with most of the major supporters.

"Did you sleep well last night?" Walt asked with a smile.

"Mostly well, but I have to admit to a few butterflies," Carl replied, matching Walt's smile. The two men reviewed the three files on the people they would be visiting that day and briefly discussed each one's history and relationship with the ministry. With time growing short, they agreed to talk further about the details of each one as they were traveling. As they prepared to leave the office, Walt turned to Carl.

"Would you like to pray for our day before we leave," Walt said, not so much asking as directing.

"Sure, Walt, I'd be happy to."

The two men folded their hands and bowed their heads.

"Gracious Lord," Carl began, "we ask for your help today so that we would do a good job presenting the needs of this ministry to these people, and we pray that you would bless our work by having them respond generously. Amen."

With that, Carl grabbed his briefcase and walked to the door. Walt took a deep breath and thought, *Dear Lord, we have a long way to go.*

The two men walked quickly to Walt's car through the cold drizzle and settled in for the drive. Walt had hardly navigated his car out of the parking lot before Carl shot him a surprising question.

"So how was it?"

"How was what?" Walt asked.

"My prayer. How was it?"

"Carl, it wasn't a test. I just wanted to be sure we prayed before we went out," Walt replied cautiously.

"Walt, I know you're concerned about how well I can integrate my faith into my work, but I want to assure you that I'm here to learn from you and that I am open to be challenged, so please don't feel like you have to pull any punches."

"Well, I appreciate your honesty, and I'll return the favor by admitting that, well, yes, I guess it was sort of a test. I apologize. Prayer shouldn't be used as an evaluation tool," Walt confessed, appreciative of Carl's open and straightforward candor.

The two drove on in a rather awkward silence for a few moments before Carl shifted the focus.

"So tell me more about Jerry Shepherd. It looks like you two have had a pretty long relationship. What are the goals for this visit?"

"I got to know Jerry on one of my first tours of our overseas programs. He had just sold his business and was interested in making a large investment in our work. He's a great guy—a lot of fun and a real man of God. I've learned a lot from Jerry over the years, and God is doing some incredible things for a lot of different ministries through him. Shoot, I introduced him to most of them, and it's really amazing to see the impact he's had."

Carl shot Walt a confused look.

"Did you say you introduced Jerry to other ministries?"

"Yeah. When I found out some of the things that were on his heart, I connected him with the development officers at three or four other ministries that aligned with his interests," Walt responded casually.

"Wow, that's pretty surprising. I guess I can't quite understand why you would introduce a ministry partner to a competitor."

Walt didn't say anything for several moments. He wanted Carl to think about his comment and see if he would come back with an adjustment to his perspective. He didn't.

"I don't think we have any competitors," Walt finally responded. "That's something that took me a while to understand, that we are all serving the kingdom of God. I think by introducing Jerry to these other ministries, I helped serve God's kingdom in a greater way, don't you?"

"Maybe," Carl replied, hoping not to sound too critical, "but what about the needs of Hands of Love? The money that Jerry ended up giving to these other ministries could have gone to us. Shouldn't that be our primary concern?"

"You know, Carl, one of the big pieces of my conversion was the shift in my thinking from a scarcity mentality to an abundance mentality," Walt replied. "Some very wise people helped me understand that there is no scarcity of resources for funding all of God's work, there is only a scarcity of people whose hearts are rich toward God."

"What do you mean conversion?" Carl asked, seeming to have missed the scarcity/abundance comment.

"Well, I don't use the word lightly. What has happened to me—my heart, my thinking, my whole view and attitude toward this work—I can only describe it as a pretty radical conversion. You might call it a transformation from where I was when I began seventeen years ago. And it's not a done deal. I'm still thinking and processing a lot of this through. It's so fundamentally different than the way I was taught to think about fundraising. Even the term had to be changed. We stopped talking about 'raising funds' and started to define our work as 'raising up faithful stewards.'"

"I did notice that. I guess I thought it was just clever wording."

"I hope not. It's all part of this conversion we're going through. You know, after all these years of trying to put it into practice, I still find myself slipping back into old patterns of thought and old ways of doing things. It has been and continues to be quite a journey, and I absolutely love it," Walt said with a smile and an unmistakable sense of conviction.

Carl wanted to hear more about this journey, but he was

anxious to be sure they were on the same page during their visit with Jerry. He didn't want to mess up on this first call with his new boss, so he was eager to return to the strategy for their meeting.

"Well, I have to think about that some more. But back to Jerry, what was the amount of his last gift? What are you planning to ask him for?" Carl asked.

"Jerry has given us around ten thousand dollars about this same time every year. He tends to designate some of his gift to a particular project and leave some for us to use as we see fit."

"So," Carl said slowly, thinking through his strategy, "if he has been giving this amount for several years, do we plan on asking him to increase it this year?"

"Well, I will ask Jerry to give what God puts on his heart to give. I have two projects to present to him that I know he'll enjoy supporting, and I always let him know how much we appreciate the undesignated portion of his giving. There's a lot of opportunity here for him to give as much as he feels led to give. It may be another ten thousand or it may be significantly more," Walt said, allowing a bit of a pause before adding the kicker, "or less."

Carl responded quickly. "Given the pressures of our budget, we can't afford for it to be less. How about we ask him to pray about an increased gift of fifteen thousand dollars this year?" he offered, trying to sound confident.

Walt turned up Magnolia Boulevard and drove along the tree-lined street that offered spectacular views across Puget Sound onto the Olympic Mountains to the west, downtown Seattle to the south, and Mount Rainier looming beyond it. Soon they pulled into the driveway of a beautifully landscaped but somewhat modest home. Walt shut the engine off, looked at his watch, acknowledged that they were a few minutes early, and turned to reply to Carl.

"Jerry has the ability to give a substantial gift to us, and I'm confident that at the right time God will place it on his heart for him to give that gift. My strategy is to keep Jerry informed of our work and the opportunities that are available for support, and then to let God do in his heart what God will do. After all, God is the fundraiser, not me."

With that comment, and without giving Carl the chance to respond, Walt gathered his things, got out of the car, and headed up the walkway.

God is the fundraiser. What does that mean? Carl thought as they approached the front door. They were immediately greeted by a smiling, energetic man in his early sixties. He thrust his hand out toward Walt and, just before he went to shake it, pulled it back and embraced Walt while letting out a joyful laugh.

"Walt, how are you, my friend? Thanks for taking the time to come by the house. I really appreciate it."

"Jerry, visiting you is one of the highlights of my month, and you know it. You look great. Are you back on your bicycle?" Walt asked smiling.

"Absolutely. Every day like clockwork. I think it saved my life," Jerry responded as they moved through the front door.

"That's great to hear Jerry. We want you around for a while. Hey Jerry, I'd like you to meet my new associate, Carl Burns. Carl, this is Jerry Shepherd."

For the next half hour the three men toured Jerry's new back deck and talked about his recovery from bypass surgery, his daughter's engagement, and his two new business deals. The conversation was warm, personal, and at times even intimate in both content and tone. Carl could tell that Jerry and Walt had been through a lot together in their relationship over the years. He was surprised at how much Jerry knew about Walt, and it seemed at times as if Jerry was leading the discussion, which made Carl nervous. They were losing control of the meeting, and their time was limited. Carl thought of jumping in and pulling the conversation back to the presentation, but it naturally shifted that direction before he could. Walt gracefully transitioned to a talk about the two projects he had brought for Jerry to review.

"This is amazing work," Jerry said, paging through the project summaries. "Hands of Love has come a long way since we were visiting those first health clinics in Somalia."

"Yes, but we've stayed true to the mission, and that's why I think we've been so blessed to have loyal partners over the years," Walt replied. "By the way, Mike wanted me to express his appreciation to you when I saw you."

Mike Pollard was the President of Hands of Love, and he and Jerry had traveled together the previous year.

"That's nice. I appreciate that. Please tell him hello for me when you see him," Jerry replied.

Carl was taking this in, trying to manage his impatience. He knew the moment for "the ask" was at hand, and he was anxious for Walt to close the deal.

Walt sat forward and spoke directly.

"Jerry, you have been a wonderful friend of Hands of Love, and your support has meant a great deal to us. These are two projects I knew you would enjoy seeing, and if you don't have any other questions, I would like to ask you to pray about these needs and let us know how God is leading you. You know, Jerry, I want you to be blessed by what you choose to give."

And with that, Walt sat back in his chair and was silent.

That was it? Carl thought. *Is that really all he is going to say?*

Jerry paged carefully through a few more items before setting the files down on the coffee table. He paused for a moment, and then looked at Walt.

"I want to do all I can for you this year, but you know how the recession has impacted us. I will certainly pray over these projects, and I know God will lead me to give as generously as I can. When do you need an answer?"

"Can you let us know by the end of the month? It would help a lot with our project planning," Walt replied.

"Yes, no problem. Probably before then, but definitely by the end of the month," Jerry said.

"If I don't hear back from you, I will give you a call, just in case life gets in the way."

"In other words, you know where I live," Jerry said with a laugh.

With that, they were up and to the door for goodbyes. Before Carl could think, they were back in the car and heading up Magnolia Boulevard.

"So, how do you think that went?" Walt asked.

Carl was careful to think through his reply. He didn't want to sound rude, but he also wanted to be honest.

"Not well, I would say. I mean, we did get an ask in, sort of, but I think he was interested enough that if we had asked him for fifteen thousand…well, I think he would have made a pledge of more than ten thousand if we had asked him directly. Now we aren't sure what he'll give." He paused and then added, "I guess I think we might have missed an opportunity, Walt."

He was hoping not to offend, but his frustration came through.

"Well, Carl, I think you are right, at least in part. Had we pressed Jerry, I think he would have given us a commitment for a gift, possibly more than ten thousand. And you're correct that we don't know what he will give and also that we gave up control by not pressing and not knowing. All of that is absolutely true," Walt said in an even and unemotional tone. "But let me ask you, what is your bottom line for a visit to a ministry partner?"

Carl knew this was one of those critical moments in a new relationship with a boss, and he didn't want to mess it up, but he also wanted to be absolutely honest in his reply. After all, he had been doing this work successfully for over a decade.

"For me, Walt, the bottom line is getting a gift. That's what we're paid to do. Now I also believe we need to develop good relationships with our supporters and be sure they know we are grateful for their support, but if we build relationships and never get a gift, I think we've failed."

Walt thought for a minute before replying.

"So generating revenue is our bottom line?" he asked flatly.

"Well, yes, when it comes down to it, we're hired to generate the funds Hands of Love needs to operate. That's pretty basic. That *is* what we're hired to do, isn't it?" Carl asked somewhat pointedly.

Walt ignored the direct question.

"So if we are hired to generate revenue, does it matter how we do it?" he asked.

"Of course," Carl replied, trying not to sound defensive. "Just because we measure success in dollars and cents doesn't mean we can be dishonest or manipulative in the process. We are working for the Lord, here. I understand that. But it doesn't change in my mind the basic fact that our job is to raise money."

Carl was frustrated that Walt seemed to be implying that if someone believed the job of a fundraiser was to raise funds, somehow that required the use of devious methods and questionable practices. He had heard this line of reasoning before, and he rejected it outright. Now he feared that Walt might go down that same path, and Carl was unnerved by the thought.

"So what is it that keeps us from using manipulation in our work, if in the end it helps us achieve our goal?" Walt asked.

We are *going down this path!* Carl thought. *Well, if that's where Walt wants to go, I will oblige.*

"Walt, I really reject the notion that you have to be manipulative if you measure your success in bottom line income. I was pretty successful raising millions of dollars at St. Luke's, and I don't believe I ever manipulated anyone to give. Do you really think that you can't have the one without the other?" Carl asked sharply.

"Let me try to answer that by going back and giving you my reply to the question I asked you earlier. My measurement, or bottom line for evaluating whether a meeting with a supporter was successful or not is simply this: Was the person blessed by our time together, and were they invited to make a true steward decision that will bless them in return? The conversion I mentioned earlier started when I took this on as my ultimate measurement of success."

Walt paused to let the idea sit for a minute with Carl.

"I don't see how being a blessing equates to raising the money that Hands of Love needs to carry out its work," Carl shot back.

"You see, Carl," Walt replied in a graceful tone, "I believe that every interaction with supporters—and this holds true for a colleague, a friend, or a family member—is an opportunity to be used by God to help them on the journey they are traveling with Christ. If I can be a blessing in their life, I have served God well. Even better, if I can be used by God to be the means by which they can receive abundant blessings from God, then Wow! How great is that? I believe when Jerry makes his decision to give, it will be in obedience to what God lays on his heart. When he does, he will be blessed with the joy of not only having obeyed, but in seeing his money—no that's wrong—in seeing *God's* money used to support God's work. My job is to create an opportunity for Jerry to be blessed like that, regardless of how much he gives."

Carl was silent as he pondered Walt's words. His defensiveness was beginning to crack as he considered what it would mean if he actually saw his work as bringing blessing into peoples' lives. That idea was staggering in its implications. He decided to stay silent and let Walt continue, for he sensed that the lesson was not over.

Walt changed lanes and then continued speaking.

"Carl, to base my success on getting the largest gift possible and getting it today, I have to shift my focus from how I can be a blessing to Jerry to how Jerry can be a blessing to me. When I do that, I start using words that are very different, words that try to convince or produce guilt or push a little to get a more immediate decision. That brings me right to the edge of manipulation, and I confess, maybe that's just my own weakness. But I've just never been able to reconcile the desire to be a blessing and bring blessing to peoples' lives with measuring my success by the size of the gifts they give. Sorry, that's kind of a long answer, but does that make sense?"

Carl was stunned by Walt's words, and he had no ready response. He had never in his professional career heard or considered that his job was to be a blessing and bring blessing into the lives of the supporters he visited. At first he pushed back hard against the idea, but the thought of that singular goal struck something deep inside him. He knew Walt was awaiting an answer, so he struggled for a reasoned reply.

"Yes, I guess so, but I have to think about that. I'll be honest. It's absolutely foreign to me. I can't even imagine how to evaluate it as a bottom line goal. Wow, Walt, that's a real zinger to me. Sorry I can't be more articulate in my response."

"Absolutely no problem, Carl. For me it was a radical shift in my entire view of our work, and it was only the first step. The more I walked down this path, the more my head began to spin. It kind of un-anchors all of your moorings for this work. That's what I meant when I talked about my conversion."

Walt's comments gave Carl some time to think, and also to find some loopholes in Walt's position.

"So how do Mike and the Board feel about this approach?

They seem like pretty bottom line people to me. Last week you sent me a report that talked about how critical this quarter was to our budget and set out some pretty challenging income goals for you…and me. Those seemed like clear financial measurements of success. How do you square all of that with your bottom line goal?" he asked.

"Great question, but we'll need to take it up after our visit with Steve and Kathy…Ortlund, I believe. Would you grab their file? We need to review their background. I've only spoken with them briefly at the September banquet," Walt said.

Carl pulled the file from his briefcase and paged through it. He shared the vital statistics with Walt. They were a young professional couple, invited by a board member to the banquet, very positive response to the work, filled out a card and checked that they would be open to learning more. A few notes from the board member indicated that they had reasonable means and that Steve was in a fast-growing company that would position him well to be a future major supporter.

"This sounds promising," Carl said. "If we can start them into a giving pattern with us, we should be able to build their support toward the major gift level in a few years."

"Getting a first gift will be critical, and hopefully we can involve them on a tour sometime soon. That's a great way to experience this ministry," Walt added. "Which reminds me, we need to get *you* on a tour so that you can see our work firsthand. Let's be sure to talk about this and get something on the schedule."

"Thanks. I would love that," Carl replied.

They arrived at the Ortlund home right on time, and Walt paused for a brief prayer before they left the car.

"Father, help us to be a blessing and use us to bring a blessing to this couple by the power of the Holy Spirit and in the name of Christ, our Lord, Amen."

CONFLICT

S teve and Kathy Ortlund were a stereotypical professional
couple in their earlier forties, complete with an upscale,
nicely kept home, three well-behaved children, and a golden
retriever named Max. They had made arrangements for the kids
and the dog to be taken care of so that they could give full attention to the two men from HOLI.

Carl and Walt positioned themselves on an overstuffed
leather couch that faced the large-paned windows looking over
the beautiful waters of Puget Sound, replete with large green
and white car ferries, sailboats, and heavily forested islands that
dotted the "the Sound," as locals called it. After some polite conversation, Walt moved the discussion to their meeting at the
banquet.

"I would be interested to know what you thought of our
speaker," Walt queried.

Steve barely beat Kathy to the reply, and she smiled and let
him continue.

"I thought Dr. Stanton was pretty provocative. Kathy and I talked a lot about it on the way home. We really expected a more direct report on the work of the ministry, but he was certainly challenging."

Kathy jumped in by asking, "Does Hands of Love usually have banquet speakers who bring such a spiritual message rather than talk more about your work?"

"No, not usually," Walt replied. "But we chose Dr. Stanton for just that reason. We felt that we wanted our friends and supporters to be challenged and built up spiritually by the speaker. We thought the video and the presentation by Mike offered enough information about the ministry. So would you agree with that?"

Steve and Kathy looked at each other for a moment, then Steve replied, "Yes, when you put it that way, I think so. We did appreciate the spiritual message, and I think we learned a lot from it."

"I don't think I'd change it, now that I think about it," Kathy added. "After all, it's what you are all about, and you have great materials that talk about the work overseas. No, I think I liked it."

Carl decided to chime in and see if he could get the discussion focused on the projects they came to discuss.

"I wish I had been there. It sounds like it was a great event. Was there anything in the presentation of the projects that struck a chord with your own interests?"

"Yes, I really appreciated your work with the Muslim population in Indonesia. I know how hard that work must be, and I was so impressed with the dedication of your field staff," Kathy replied.

"That's got to be incredibly hard work," Steve added.

"Yes," Walt said, "I had the privilege of visiting their work last year with a small group of our ministry partners, and we were all blown away by the dedication of those staff members. Tell me, do you support other work with Muslims?"

Steve responded, "Yes, we've been giving to International Islamic Outreach, a ministry through our denomination."

"Oh yes, I've heard of them. Wonderful ministry. I'm glad you're supporting them," Walt said enthusiastically—a little too enthusiastically for Carl. He hoped Walt would get back to *their* projects and move to an ask.

"I would be interested to know, if this is not too personal to ask, where you have experienced your greatest joy as a financial supporter of different ministries?" Walt asked, leaning forward and indicating his keen interest in their answer.

"Wow," Kathy replied, looking at Steve questioningly, "that is quite a question. I'm not sure I expected that one." Her tone was not one of accusation but one of genuine intrigue.

The two thought for a moment, and then Steve said something quietly to Kathy, who nodded in agreement. He looked at Walt and replied, "Honestly, I wish we had more joy in our giving. We are so busy that most of our giving decisions are made on the fly. We give to our church pretty regularly, but beyond that it is mostly hit and miss as needs arise. This sounds terrible to say, but," Steve looked carefully at Kathy, who gave him an approving nod, "I don't think we really get a lot of joy from our giving."

"There's a true confession," Kathy said with a laugh that was quickly shared by Steve and Walt. "It's a great question, Walt. We'll need to think on that some more," she added.

"You know," Walt said, "if you are interested, I have a wonderful article I came across a few months ago that talks about this very thing: how we get so busy that we miss out on the joy God has for us when we are obedient to his will. I'll send it to you as an email attachment. Let me know if it's helpful."

"Thanks, Walt," they said in near unison.

Carl was growing increasingly impatient. They had been there almost forty-five minutes and still no direct talk about a proposal and no ask.

Walt continued, "I want you to know early on in this relationship how important it is to me and the staff at HOLI that you be blessed in every way that you interact with our ministry. That includes any financial support you may choose to give."

The comment struck deeply with both Steve and Kathy. As a caring couple with growing financial resources, they had experienced the parade of well-intentioned fundraisers who had sat right where Walt and Carl were sitting and who, once the niceties were over, jumped directly in to what they wanted to get from them. To Steve and Kathy, it was clear from the start that they were being sold. They usually would give a small amount to get the evening over with. That had a lot to do with their inability to answer Walt's question about joyful giving. They almost canceled this meeting because of so many previous bad experiences in which they felt they were being used and manipulated in order to get a gift. But there was something about Walt's approach at the banquet and in his follow-up calls that put them at ease, and now they were beginning to understand what it was.

Unfortunately, about that time Carl's patience had run out.

Walt paused to let the last comment sink in, and Carl grabbed his chance.

"Steve, Kathy, we believe that you value the work of Hands of Love and understand the importance of our work. Would you be prepared tonight to consider a gift of one thousand dollars or more to support the work in Indonesia we discussed earlier?"

Walt was stunned. Steve and Kathy suddenly felt thrust back into those previous meetings that they wanted to avoid. Steve shot Walt a look of surprise and, without even looking at Kathy, replied flatly, "sure, I guess we could do that."

Walt jumped back in, "Steve, that's very generous, thank you, thank you both. I want you to know that as important as every gift is to support our work, what matters most is ensuring that you are blessed by your decision to give as God leads."

It was a noble try, but the environment had changed dramatically in a few short seconds. Steve and Kathy were clearly working to control their agitation at the turn that the conversation had taken. Their facial expressions and body language told the story. Steve stood up, indicating that the visit was over, and his closing remarks cut Walt deeply.

"I will get a check to you in the mail. Thanks for coming by. We appreciate the visit."

Carl sensed the tension, but was pleased with the outcome. He replied, "Great, Steve. We appreciate your support, and we look forward to getting together again."

Kathy rose, shook their hands, and gave them an obligatory smile. With that, Walt and Carl were soon out the door.

Once they got into the car, Carl jumped right into discussion.

"Well, we got what we came for. I hope it was okay for me to make the ask. We were running short on time, and I thought I might support you by getting to the close. I know a thousand isn't a lot for them, but it's a good start. Just what we hoped for, right?" Carl asked with a little bit of hesitancy in his voice.

Walt backed the car out and started down the street, trying to form his response in a way that could help Carl understand.

"Carl, what we got was a transaction. Steve will write a check. We'll deposit it. End of story. That's what we got. That's *all* we got."

"I don't agree. I think we opened up the opportunity to go back to them for future gifts, hopefully larger gifts. They were very interested in our needs," Carl insisted.

"But Carl, we showed them that we weren't interested in theirs," Walt shot back. "We had the opportunity to help them recover the real joy of giving in a God-pleasing way, to develop hearts that are rich toward God and to be blessed in their giving. Now all we have is a transactional gift and a closed door to minister to them any further. No, Carl, we didn't get what we came for."

The two rode on in silence for quite a while before Carl spoke. He had been trying to reconcile his well-honed instincts for fundraising with Walt's strange way of thinking about the whole profession. Dejected and confused, Carl spoke openly to Walt.

"Walt, I apologize if I took the discussion in the wrong direction. I honestly don't know if I can do this. All of my training and instincts tell me that we got a good outcome, that what

I said was the right thing to say. I'm just not sure I can make the magnitude of change in my approach that you're asking. I'm not sure I even understand what that change looks like."

Walt appreciated the openness and the sincere frustration Carl was feeling. It was reminiscent of Walt's own difficult journey. He surprised Carl with his reply.

"Carl, I know this is a fundamental change from all your experience has taught you. I don't expect this to be easy, but please don't give up. Let me ask you something. How would you answer the question I asked Steve and Kathy?"

Carl thought back and wondered just which question Walt was referring to. Before he could ask, Walt clarified, "The question about where you have experienced your greatest joy as a financial supporter of different ministries?"

Carl was taken aback by the question in the same way the Ortlunds were. He and Cheryl were pretty good givers, but no one had ever asked them that question. Carl had to think about it for several moments. In doing so he realized that his response would not sound too much different from Steve and Kathy's. He received a sense of satisfaction when he was able to help a ministry, but he honestly never remembered real joy. More often than not, they just wrote checks without thinking too much about it.

"I can't say Cheryl and I are in much of a different place than Steve and Kathy. I enjoy giving, and I think we are pretty generous, but it's all, well, automatic. We don't really talk or think about it much, so I can't say I can point to any real sense of joy in any of our giving. Wow, I guess that really is a confession," he said, hoping to get a reaction from Walt.

"Why do you think that is? I mean, what causes us to turn

giving into a routine like that?" Walt asked with a genuinely caring tone.

"I don't know. I guess it just hasn't been important enough for me to think it through more carefully," Carl guessed.

"No, I don't think that's what it is. I do think it is important to you and Cheryl, and to Steve and Kathy. I think there may be another reason. I think it may be that it's easy for us to forget that it really isn't our money to begin with. I know that when I was confronted on this idea, I realized that I took giving for granted because I considered it my money to do with as I wished. Oh, I knew better conceptually. I knew that everything belonged to God, at least I gave that truth lip service, but I lived as though I owned it all and could therefore make giving decisions without much thought or prayer. Once I became convinced that all I had really *was* God's, I was forced to take a very different approach to how I chose to give it, and spend it."

Carl nodded his head slowly.

"You know, Walt, you're right. I don't really consider God's ownership like I should. I mean, I *know it,* I just don't put it into practice very well."

"And that's why you don't know the joy of being a godly steward," Walt replied. "And neither did I. I missed out on so much joy all those years playing the owner and pretending I was lord over my own little kingdom."

"I'm not sure what you mean," Carl said.

"When I became a Christian, I intended to give my whole life to Christ. I mean, I wanted nothing held back. That's what I call one-kingdom living, and that's what I wanted. One lord, one life, one-kingdom: *his* kingdom. Can you relate?" Walt asked.

"Sure, that's what Cheryl and I both want for us and for our kids. But that's hard to do perfectly all the time."

"Nearly impossible, I would say. I don't know how it is for you and Cheryl, but Marie and I had to acknowledge that there were chunks of our life that we held back from giving over to God's control. One of those chunks was our finances, and that's a hard thing to admit as a professional fundraiser.

"We got caught up in that automatic giving mode for a long time before someone asked me the same question I asked you. That started Marie and I on a journey that continues today. It's a process of daily laying down everything we have and everything we are before God, full submission and nothing less. And it's hard," Walt said, shaking his head.

"But I'll bet you can answer that question now. Am I right?" Carl asked.

Walt smiled in appreciation of the olive branch.

"Yes, I can truly say that I can. Marie and I began rethinking our entire attitude toward our money, and later we added our time, our relationships, our self-images, even our relationship to God. We began to see that we are only stewards of all of these relationships. We really don't own anything at all, *nothing*," Walt said emphatically.

"Ashes to ashes and dust to dust," Carl added.

"Exactly! And the more we embraced our total lack of ownership of anything, the more we began to experience a sense of freedom we had never known. That's when I began to understand the reason we had never known the real joy of giving was because we had never been set free to give as faithful stewards. Owners can never be joyful givers, because they aren't free."

"So you're saying that Steve and Kathy needed to be set free," Carl offered.

"A lot more than we needed a thousand dollars," Walt replied, trying to soften the blow of the words. "We had the chance to be used by God to help them understand their owner-ship approach to life, and maybe, just maybe, to watch the Spirit of God set them free. It wouldn't have happened tonight, but over time, with the right relationship and lots of prayer, it most likely would."

"And now, likely never," Carl replied with contrition in his voice.

"Well, we don't know that. God has a lot of resources to reach the Ortlunds."

"But it won't be us. I'm really sorry, Walt. This is all so new to me."

"It's okay, Carl. But if you take away anything from this day so far, please consider these two things. First, our goal is to be a blessing to those who support this ministry and to provide opportunities for God to bless them. Second, our mission as development professionals is to be used by God to help set peo-ple free. That's a lot for one day, but that is what I pray you con-sider as your calling at HOLI."

OLD WOUNDS

W alt pulled into the parking lot of a glass high-rise tower that sat amidst a block of similar corporate structures. He and Carl had been so wrapped up in their conversation they didn't realize until they saw the office complex that they had reached the location of their final visit of the day. Walt parked the car, and they pulled out the file on Jack Meacham.

"Jack is one of my more challenging relationships," Walt said. "He used to be on the board but left because he felt it was run too inefficiently and wasn't a good use of his time. He runs the Meacham Global Fund. It's a major mutual fund company that has done pretty well, even through the recession. He told me once that he employed over four hundred people at the height of the market. He's down some, but he still has substantial personal wealth."

Carl reviewed the documentation on Jack and his own notes from earlier in the day. "His giving is pretty sporadic: three thousand, then fifteen thousand, and then almost nothing."

Walt nodded.

"Jack gives for only two reasons: tax benefits and guilt."

"Guilt?" Carl asked. He could understand a businessman being concerned about the tax advantages of giving, but guilt?

"Jack is twice divorced, both times from the same woman, Sally. Sally is a long-time friend of Hands of Love, and she's now one of our staffers in India. Jack blames himself for both divorces, especially the second one. It's a long story, but suffice it to say that Jack gives to us mostly as a guilt offering to appease his conscience about having driven Sally away. Since we don't raise designated funds for field staff, he feels like he is still giving to support her when he gives to the ministry," Walt explained.

Carl thought for a moment, and then he said something that surprised himself and greatly pleased Walt.

"Walt, we have to be careful here. This is a situation that is rife for manipulation. I can see how easy it would be to play on those guilt feelings to get a bigger amount from Jack. We have to be careful not to go there, don't we?" He emphasized the *we* to let Walt know he was mostly talking about himself.

Walt smiled.

"Carl, you nailed it. That's what I battle every time I come to see Jack. In the back of my mind I know I have this powerful card that I can play…and Jack knows it, too."

Carl hesitated before asking the obvious question. He didn't want to pretend to be holding Walt accountable, especially in this area that was so new to him and so deeply ingrained in Walt. But his curiosity got the better of him.

"So, have you ever played the guilt card with him?"

Walt looked at him a bit surprised, and then he looked down and shook his head slowly while drawing a deep breath.

"I am sorry to say that I have—only once—but yes."

Carl wasn't sure if Walt would say any more, so he sat quietly. Walt slowly told the story.

"We were four days from the end of our fiscal year and we desperately needed one hundred and fifteen thousand dollars more to end in the black. Programs and staff were on the chopping block, and Jack was one of only three serious sources I could go to in hopes of raising that kind of money. I planned on approaching it with him like I always had, encouraging him to pray about it carefully and make a gift that would bring him joy and blessing. He had never done that in all my years of asking."

He paused for a moment to lament what he had just said.

"In our conversation," he continued, "Jack told me that he had just sold a side business that had netted him seven figures, almost eight. I knew he was sitting on a lot of cash, and a gift the size I needed would be easy for him to make. I shared our need for the full amount and asked him to pray about it, which he said he would—though we both knew he wouldn't. But that shouldn't have mattered. It was my moment to trust God and believe that he would work through Jack, or someone else, to supply our needs.

"You know, Carl, I can remember the exact moment my flesh grabbed me. I thought about how wonderful it would be to go back to the office with a one hundred and fifteen thousand dollar check, how happy everyone would be and how good I would look after saving the day. So, after Jack had agreed to pray about it, I looked straight at him and without blinking an eye I told him that if we did not raise the funds by Friday, a lot of staff positions would be cut…especially in India."

The pain of that moment was clear on Walt's face as he grimaced and shook his head.

"You know Walt, twenty-four hours ago, if you had told me that story, I would have said, 'Great move. That was brilliant!' Now I find myself wincing at the thought. So, is this the start of this conversion you've been talking about?" Carl asked with a grin.

The comment brought Walt out of his painful memory and generated a broad smile.

"Yes, I think it is," he said back to Carl.

As the two men entered the building, they talked briefly about how best to approach Jack, given this history. They agreed that they would continue to encourage Jack to give prayerful consideration of a gift, and Carl gave Walt his word that he would focus on being a blessing to Jack instead of getting a gift. They were up the elevator to the eleventh floor and into the opulent office of the Meacham Global Fund.

Walt and Carl introduced themselves to a perky receptionist and took a seat in the waiting area. Before long, Jack appeared. He was pretty much what Carl expected: mid-fifties, in a starched white shirt, red checked tie, and what must have been a two thousand dollar suit. He had the look of a financial professional, and his demeanor was cordial but not overly warm.

"Good afternoon, Walt. It's good to see you again," Jack said with a half smile. "This must be your new associate," he said while offering a handshake to Carl that seemed more obligatory than genuine.

Walt introduced Carl to Jack as the three of them walked back to his office. As Carl expected, Jack's office occupied the large corner space with spectacular views out two directions. They sat around a small conference table. Jack's assistant brought them coffee as they began their conversation.

"So how are things at the organization?" Jack asked Walt.

"We have our usual joys and challenges, but overall I think we're moving in a very positive direction," Walt replied. "I've been following the Global Fund online, and you seem to be weathering the recession pretty well. How are you doing personally, Jack?"

Jack got up and walked over to look out one of the massive windows onto downtown Seattle and Elliott Bay. The Space Needle stood squarely in front of the main window, and the Olympic Mountains made occasional appearances through the clouds across Puget Sound. He took several moments before answering, and then turned back to the pair seated at the conference table.

"It's been a tough year, tougher than I would've expected—even with the bad economic news. We're pretty diversified here, by intention. We try to anticipate these downturns and help our clients survive them. Overall, certainly compared to a lot of our competitors, I guess we've done pretty well. But it's just hard to get a lot of satisfaction out of holding your own. I guess it's a sign of the times, but I'm sure looking forward to getting back to the chance to make double-digit returns. I just hope those times come back," Jack said, almost talking to himself.

Walt leaned forward.

"And how have *you* been, Jack, through all this?"

Jack looked straight at Walt with an expression that showed that he was not surprised by the question.

"Thanks for asking. I knew you would. I try to be philosophical about these times. I know they won't last, and so I just try to hold on and make good decisions, keep morale high, and wait."

"They that wait upon the Lord will renew their strength," Walt replied. "I suppose that has special meaning in times like this."

"Well, it should," Jack said in a confessional tone. "You know, Walt, I've always struggled with integrating my faith and my work. I'm not sure I know if God is even interested in all this mutual fund stuff." He then looked directly at Carl and asked, "Do *you* think he is?"

Carl's heart rate spiked as he was suddenly brought into this intimate conversation at a critical moment. He thought quickly and tried to come up with an answer that would be an honest response to Jack that fit into this new fundraising paradigm he was learning from Walt. He drew a deep breath and waded in.

"Yes, Jack, I do. Over my career, I have talked with hundreds of successful business leaders and most believed that there was no separation between their lives as Christians and their vocation as business leaders. They all integrated those in different ways, but I've always been amazed and grateful at how many understood that God cares about everything we do."

Jack thought for a minute. Walt decided to keep quiet and let this conversation and relationship between Jack and Carl continue. Jack looked back at Carl and replied.

"Yeah, I suppose you're right. Sometimes this seems like such a secular, worldly profession that I wouldn't blame him if he didn't care how it went. It's not like your work where everything you do seems so godly. I guess I have to think about it some more, but why don't we get to the purpose of this meeting? Walt, tell me what I can do for you."

"I'll be happy to talk with you about what's happening at Hands of Love, but knowing how you are doing and being able to pray specifically for you, well, that really *is* the purpose of this meeting," Walt said.

"You know, Walt, after all these years I really do believe that, and I appreciate it. I want you to know that. Despite a few bumps in the road, your friendship means a lot to me. I always feel better about things after we've talked. So forgive me for being presumptuous. I know where your heart is," Jack replied in a warmer tone then they had first heard when they arrived.

"I do have a very short window, however, and I would like to hear more about the ministry," Jack continued.

"I understand. Let me share an update with you and tell you about a couple projects I think you may be interested in supporting," Walt replied.

For the next twenty minutes, Walt and Carl talked with Jack about the financial status at HOLI, and they presented him two proposals for projects that aligned with his own interests in their work. Jack listened carefully, asked a few pointed questions, and then sat back in his chair.

"This is all very impressive. I can't believe how much you get done with so few resources," he said while shaking his head. And then he asked the question that Walt had hoped to avoid answering: "So, how is the work going in India?"

Walt thought for a brief moment before replying.

Carl was aware that this was a moment of temptation to manipulate that he and Walt had discussed on their way to the meeting. He listened intently for how Walt would reply.

"The work is going well, Jack. We are fortunate to have a number of people interested in our work in India, and they continue to support it, even during these tough times. We've had to make a few cutbacks," Walt hesitated and chose his words carefully before continuing, "but all of our staff are still there."

Walt looked at Jack and knew that enough had been said.

"That's good to hear. Thanks, Walt. I'll certainly support you again this year. I don't have to give you the 'times are tough' spiel. But even so, I'll do what I can," Jack said as he collected the papers together and put them in a file.

Walt didn't want to leave without the opportunity to help Jack in his journey as a godly steward. He said a quick silent prayer for support.

"Jack, I pray that you will be led to give a gift that really brings you joy. Whatever amount that might be, I really want you to be blessed in this process. Is there anything I can do to help make that happen for you?" Walt asked.

Jack was already on his feet moving the file to his desk and preparing to usher his guests to the door. Walt's question caused him to pause for a minute as he stood in front of his desk. He opened the manila folder and leafed through the project proposals. Carl was on the edge of his seat wondering how Jack would reply. He was amazed that Walt had asked the question, but he began to understand more and more how that question fit with Walt's perspective of his work.

Finally, Jack looked up at Walt and Carl.

"I think you've asked me that question, or some version of it, every time we've met. I have to be honest with you, Walt. I usually just write it off. Partly because, of all the fundraising officers who come to see me, you're the only one that ever asks it. Everyone else seems pretty content just to get a check and leave."

Then Jack looked directly at Carl.

"You can learn a lot from this guy. He's the real deal."

After a short pause, Jack took a deep breath and said, "Okay, I'm going to take these proposals home. I give you my word I will pray over them and see if I get some sense from God about what I should do. I'll let you know what I hear."

Walt sensed Jack was skeptical as to whether he would receive any real direction from his prayers, but Walt was delighted with his response.

Walt and Carl met Jack on their way to the door.

"I'll definitely look forward to hearing from you," Walt said, shaking Jack's hand. Jack smiled but said nothing. He shook Carl's hand and soon they were out the door and back on the elevator.

"Amazing," Walt said shaking his head. "That's the first time he's ever said he would consider praying about his decision. Just amazing."

"And I think he meant it," Carl added.

"So do I. Now I pray that he'll sense God's leading. I can't tell you what it would mean after all these years for him to really know the joy of faithful, sacrificial giving. Dear God, help make that happen for him."

The two men drove away without much conversation. Both were reflecting on the events of the day. Walt was still shaking his head at Jack's willingness to pray over his decision. Carl was trying to piece the day together and figure out the contours of this new approach to work that he had been doing the better part of his professional life. He knew that he had blown it with the Ortlunds, a performance he never wanted to repeat, but he was still unsure about the full scope of this new approach, and even less sure about its impact on his behavior as the new Director of Stewardship for HOLI. As he was replaying the day in his mind, the story of Walt's painful meeting with Jack came back to him.

As they neared the HOLI offices, Carl turned to Walt and asked a question that had been churning in him since that earlier conversation about Jack. He didn't want to bring up a bad memory again for Walt, but he was dying to know the answer, so he decided to take a chance.

"So, how much did he end up giving?" Carl asked with some hesitancy. Walt's mind was elsewhere, so the question caught him off guard.

"How much did *who* end up giving?" he asked.

"Jack. You said you mentioned closing offices in India where Sally was. Did Jack give you the full amount you needed?" Carl asked as gracefully as he could.

Walt continued to stare out ahead and drive on until they came to a stoplight.

"Yes, yes he did," Walt responded with a sigh. "Right then and there he pulled out his checkbook and wrote out the most joyless, disgusted gift I have ever witnessed. He practically tore the whole checkbook when he ripped it out and handed it to me.

He didn't even look at me. He just thrust the check toward me. I thanked him, but I knew I had taken our relationship back to the beginning. All the trust and my chance to be a witness to him were gone. But I had my stupid check," Walt said, letting some of the anger that still resided in him show through.

"I went to my other two appointments and could barely get through them. My conscience was too heavy. I actually dreaded the thought of going back to the office and pulling out that check. Imagine being cheered as the hero for violating every principle on which you base your work and worth. So I didn't do it," Walt said abruptly, catching Carl completely off guard.

"What do you mean? You never went back to the office?" Carl asked.

"No, I mean, I went back to the office, but I just told everyone that people were thinking and praying, and we would know by Friday. For the next three days, I took out that check and looked at it and relived the painful memory of my manipulation. Yet the need for funds continued and the anxiety grew in the office as Friday approached."

Walt parked in the HOLI lot, shut off the car, and turned toward Carl to finish the story. Carl was on the edge of his seat as Walt continued.

"On Thursday night, Marie and I talked and prayed, and through her gracious and honest counsel, I decided to sit down with Mike first thing Friday morning, show him the check, and confess the approach I took to secure it. I did just that, and Mike and I prayed for guidance for the right thing to do. As soon as we finished praying, we looked at each other and both knew exactly what needed to happen. We hardly had to say a word.

I was down and in my car within moments. When I got to the Meacham Global Fund offices I was fortunate to find Jack there. I surprised him, and he agreed somewhat reluctantly to give me ten minutes. I sat down, took out the check, and set it in front of him. He was pretty surprised to see that I hadn't deposited it. I told him that I couldn't take it, and I opened up to him and shared my view of why people should give, the blessing of giving, and the joy I so much wanted him to know. Then I confessed my use of manipulation and asked for his forgiveness."

"That's amazing," Carl said quietly, mostly to himself.

Walt nodded. "It's something I never could've done on my own, but I sensed God's power and approval so strongly that I knew without doubt it was the right thing to do."

"So what did Jack say?" Carl asked anxiously.

"He was speechless for a moment. Then he composed himself, and in his business-like manner, he thanked me for my honesty. There was a critical moment where I knew he would either allow us to return to our previous level of openness and honesty or end both the conversation and our friendship. Fortunately, by God's grace, he told his assistant that we would need another thirty minutes. Then he went on to tell me that he had planned for that to be the last gift he would ever give to us, and the last meeting he ever cared to have with me."

"So he knew he was being manipulated," Carl replied.

"Yes, although he didn't call it that. He told me that he felt like I had put the needs of the organization ahead of our friendship, and he called it disingenuous. You know, Carl, I had never realized just how much he valued our relationship and the trust we'd built. Sometimes, with people like Jack who are so business-like, you never really know how much they value the relationship. But clearly he had, and it was the broken trust that hurt him the most. He was used to people trying to manipulate him—that's business—but he wasn't expecting that from a friend who he trusted and cared for."

"Did he take the check back?" Carl asked.

Walt nodded.

"Yep, every penny of it. And it was like a great weight was lifted off my shoulders. Imagine losing the one gift that your ministry so badly needed, and feeling so incredibly relieved about it. Now that is a witness to how different this approach to our work really is. I pray you can learn from the mistakes and defeats I've experienced in my own journey down this road and save yourself a lot of grief."

"Thanks, Walt. I really appreciate your openness, but my wife will tell you that it's likely I'll be stubborn enough to have to learn a lot of these lessons the hard way for myself," he said, and they both laughed at the likelihood that Cheryl was right.

As they got out of the car and walked toward the front doors of HOLI, Carl asked one more question.

"So Walt, did the ministry make its goal without Jack's gift?"

Walt opened the doors and as they walked in he stopped in the lobby to reply.

"Actually, we did, but not in the way any of us expected. My other sources came through with about half of what we needed. On that critical Friday, a long-time staffer announced her retirement. She was in a job we did not plan to refill, but we expected her to stay another two or three years. That saved a big chunk of our budget for the next year, and we were able to shift undesignated funds that we set aside for her position in order to finish out the year in the black. It was interesting. Molly—that was the staff person's name—Molly had been praying about retiring and wondered if the financial stress at HOLI was God's way of helping her decide to retire early. When Friday came and Mike announced that the funds were still short, it was confirmation for Molly. The real witness of the hand of God in this work is this: Molly has told all of us many times since that it was the most wonderful decision she had ever made. She had four great years with Stan, her husband, before he was taken by a heart attack. She cherished those years that they had together, which they never would have had if she had stayed on with us."

"And if you had kept Jack's check and announced that you had made the budget…"

"Molly would have stayed on and lost her years with Stan," Walt said with a nod.

"Amazing story," Carl said.

"Amazing God," Walt replied, patting Carl on the back as they walked out of the lobby and back to his office.

The two men spent some time checking e-mail and phone messages and then wrapped up their papers and prepared to leave for the day.

"So, what are you going to tell Cheryl about your first day?" Walt asked with a chuckle.

"I'm not sure I know what to think myself, much less what I'm going to say to Cheryl," Carl admitted. "I can tell you I've never spent a day like this in my entire career as a fundraiser. I'm not sure I really understand it all, and it worries me a little that

I'm supposed to be providing leadership to the team here when I haven't even figured this out myself."

"That's a great place to start," Walt replied, "knowing what you don't know and being willing to figure it out for yourself. I don't want to overuse the word, but those are the next steps in this conversion process. Tonight, let me ask you to identify the most enjoyable or satisfying part of what you learned today, and also what is the biggest question you have as you reflect on all that has happened. Let's take those up in the morning. Oh, and by the way, I have a surprise for you. We're having breakfast with Mike and Peter Allison, our board chair. I thought you might like to have the opportunity to hear their perspective on this subject. Let's meet here at seven."

"That's great. Thanks, Walt. And let me think about those two assignments. We can discuss them tomorrow. Thanks for a great day. I'll see you here at seven o'clock."

Carl drove home in a distracted fog. He kept playing over and over again in his mind all of the conversations from the day. He felt like he had several pieces to a very important puzzle, but none of them fit together very well, and a number of pieces were still missing. He was relieved to see his house. He drove into the garage, put the automatic garage door down, and sat for a few minutes in his car.

What am *I going to tell Cheryl?* he thought.

NEW WINESKINS

I t was another typically gray and rainy winter day in Seattle as Carl arrived at the Hands of Love office at 6:45 am. He found Walt already in his office catching up on some unfinished business from the previous day.

"Good morning, Carl. Welcome to a beautiful day in Seattle," Walt said with a smile.

"I guess this will take some getting used to," Carl replied, shaking some of the water off his overcoat. "You do get a summer here, don't you?"

"Oh yes, absolutely, and it's spectacular. Let's see, last year I think we had it on August fifth," Walt replied laughing.

"Please don't tell Cheryl that. She's such a sun lover, and that'll definitely put her over the edge," Carl replied, joining Walt in a good laugh.

Carl poured a cup of coffee and joined Walt at his small conference table.

"So, I'm curious, how did it go talking to Cheryl about your day yesterday?" Walt asked.

"That will take a little time to explain," Carl replied. "Suffice it to say she is as curious as I am. When I told her about the Ortlund visit it really seemed to resonate deeply with her, and so did the story of our time with Jack."

"I'd like to hear more. I've found that women seem to get this a lot more quickly than we do. How about the homework I left you with? Did you decide what the most satisfying part of your day was yesterday and also what the biggest question is you have?" Walt asked.

"I'll ask you my big question after breakfast, but as for the most satisfying moment of the day yesterday, I think this will surprise you. That moment for me came as I watched Steve and Kathy think about their giving and realizing together that they really didn't have much joy in the process. Even though I was squirming like mad, wondering when you were going to get to the ask, and even though I totally screwed it up by the way I responded, I realized when I reflected back on that visit that there was a very satisfying sense of watching you help them connect with this strong realization that they weren't experiencing the joy that they should in their giving. This is such a personal process, and to be able to use our relationships to help people give more joyfully and obediently does touch something deep within me. I'm still not sure how to make that happen, and I certainly have no idea how to measure it, much less teach it or train it, but there's something very right about it. So, there's my answer."

"Wow, that's certainly not what I expected to hear," Walt replied, "but it's the issue I hoped you might be willing to struggle with. You're on the right path, Carl. C'mon, let's head to breakfast."

The two men gathered their things and then walked down the hall and out into the parking lot. As Walt was steering his Prius into the Seattle traffic, he asked Carl a follow-up question.

"How did that process with Steve and Kathy make you think about your own giving?"

"Well," Carl replied, "that's the conversation that Cheryl and I had that I need to talk with you about. It made us think a lot, and it made us pretty uncomfortable. You know we always considered ourselves generous givers, but two words we would never use to describe our giving were sacrificial and joyful. I heard you use those words several times yesterday, and I wondered why I've never considered them as important ways of describing how I should give. Cheryl pretty much agreed with me, but she took an even tougher stand. She reminded me of all the times we had made promises to ourselves that we would be more generous and how few times we actually kept those promises. It was a tough conversation. We had asked ourselves why we hadn't been more generous, and why we just didn't have much joy when we did give."

"Did you come to any conclusions?" Walt asked.

"A few, but it's definitely a conversation that'll continue. The place we focused in on the most was when I shared with her your comments about one-kingdom living. I asked her how faithful she thought we had been in giving everything we had over to Christ. I didn't like the answer. We had to admit that there were all kinds of things—all kinds of *stuff*—that we really hadn't let go of. In fact, the more we named things, the more we realized that we control most everything in our lives. You know it's funny, Walt, but it's almost as if Cheryl had been dying to have this conversation with me for years. Once I opened the door, she walked right through it. Thank God she loves me, because she was brutal."

Walt nodded in full understanding. "When I first told Marie about the two-kingdom view of life and asked her if she thought I was a two-kingdom person, you know what she said to me?" Walt asked.

"No, what?"

"She said, 'Honey, you have worn that crown so long that I'm not sure I would recognize you without it.'"

"Ouch, only a wife can say that." Carl replied. "Although, that's not too far from what Cheryl said to me last night. I never realized how much control I've tried to maintain over my life, and I also never realized how much Cheryl knew it. Like I said, when I opened the door, boy did she walk through it!"

"So, are you two okay?" Walt asked a bit concerned.

"Oh yes, definitely. In fact, we may have never been better. It was an honest and difficult conversation, but it cleared the air on a lot of issues that we had stuffed away for years. We've got a long way to go, but we came away from our time committed to figuring out what it would look like for us to really be one-kingdom people. Do you have any suggestions for us?" Carl asked.

"I have some articles that helped Marie and I, but mostly it was just lots of honest conversation like you had with Cheryl last night. It's a great start, Carl, and Marie and I will commit to keep you two in prayer as you work this through. Maybe the four of us can get together when you're comfortable talking with us about this and we can share some of our journey with you."

They arrived at the restaurant and were soon inside to greet

Mike and Peter. Carl was excited for this opportunity to spend time with the executive director and board chair. Their time was short, and he hoped someone would pave the way for the conversation. He didn't have to wait long.

"So, Carl, how was your first day on the road with this guy?" Mike asked, slapping Walt on the shoulder.

"We prayed for you," Peter said with a chuckle.

"Thanks. I'm not sure who needed it more, Walt or me," Carl replied laughing. "It was an amazing day; that's for sure. I learned a lot, made a couple of stupid mistakes, and came away with more questions than answers. Walt's a great teacher, but I need to be honest with you that this is a new perspective for me. I just hope I can do the kind of job you want me to do for Hands of Love."

"Thanks for being honest with us," Mike replied. "But that really doesn't surprise us. I want you to know, Carl, that we're one hundred percent behind you, so take your time to listen and learn from Walt. None of us expect you to make this conversion overnight."

There was that word again: *conversion.* Carl was surprised to hear Mike use it, and he began to understand that this new way of thinking about fundraising had become part of the culture of the entire organization. But he still had some serious questions.

"Thanks for the support, Mike, I really appreciate it. Do you guys mind if I ask you a couple of direct questions based on what happened yesterday?" Carl asked.

"Fire away," Peter replied.

"I think I can understand this whole approach to seeing our work as being a blessing to the ministry partners that we meet, and how helping them to become more generous givers is our way of bringing blessing into their lives. I think I get that, and it resonates at a real personal level. What I don't get is how we measure it. How I am supposed to train for it and hold people accountable in the work they do? Can you help me?" Carl asked.

Peter looked at Mike and Mike nodded back to Peter to provide an answer.

"That's a great question. It's one that I still wrestle with, and I think you'll find that's true for the rest of the board. When Walt first introduced us to this concept, that question was the question of the day. We wanted to embrace this approach because it so aligns with scripture and our personal faith journeys, but it seemed so impractical!" Peter admitted.

"The board didn't know how to measure it, and I didn't know how to manage Walt to help him be successful in carrying it out," Mike added. "The breakthrough for us came when we were challenged to consider that if we were faithful in *how* we carried out our work of raising up faithful stewards we could trust that God would be faithful in *what* that work produced. So we began to figure out how to measure, train, and budget for the *how*."

Peter then picked up the response.

"I can still remember the day when we shared with the board that we were going to begin measuring our success in fundraising based solely on activity and not outcome. We would set clear expectations for the productivity of our development team based on the time spent in building relationships, initiating new relationships, and clearly and honestly presenting the needs of the ministry. At that point, we would trust God for the increase. It meant we had to rethink our entire budgeting process so that we could spend what we raised and not commit to spend what we projected we *might* raise. We no longer sent out our development team with a goal they had to meet in order for us to carry out our work, but we prepared our program people to be flexible and able to initiate and carry out work in the field based on the level to which God blessed the work of our development team. So we developed program plans and budgets with field staff and then the development team put those in front of our ministry supporters. What they felt led to fund is what we implemented in the field. It was a significant reversal in the way we had done things for the past thirty-two years."

"And how did the board respond?" Carl asked.

"Some liked it, some reserved judgment, and a few left the board. Since then we have rebuilt the board with people who embrace it, and it has helped that this approach has proven itself over and over again," Peter replied.

"It's required an entire cultural shift in our organization, but none of us would ever go back now," Mike added.

"Now you can see why I feel I have the full freedom to leave the final giving decision to the prayerful consideration of our ministry partners," Walt interjected. "I couldn't do this if I didn't have the support of Mike, Peter, and the board. We all believe this is the most God-honoring way to do our work, but it's taken a long time and a pretty difficult process of shifting our culture to where this is now the expectation. It had to be integrated throughout our development work. That means our direct mail, events, even the way we acknowledge gifts. It's also had an amazing effect on the level of support we get from our own staff and board."

"Last year we had one hundred percent of all employees and board members give financially to support the ministry. I never thought I'd see the day when that would happen, and with no coercion either," Mike said with a chuckle.

"So let me see if I have this straight," Carl said. "My job is to set goals based on levels of activity that include building good relationships with current ministry partners, starting relationships with new potential ministry partners, and putting a well crafted case for support in front of all of them. If I do that successfully, and can train and manage our staff to do the same, the board will support us regardless of how much money that work produces?"

"Almost," Mike replied. "The one missing piece is your responsibility to ensure that you and all of your team members are prepared each day to carry out this work in a God-honoring way. It's so easy to slip back into old habits and patterns of raising money. A big part of your job is helping your staff grow in their skill set and progress along the journey they are on in their faith."

"It almost sounds like I'm expected to be a pastor as much as a team leader," Carl said hesitantly.

"I'm not sure a pastor is quite what we have in mind, but you are responsible to shepherd your team effectively, and that includes their spiritual preparation and development. It may be the most critical role you play, because if we get that wrong, everything else falls apart," Peter replied.

"That's why I pressed you so hard on this subject during the interview," Walt interjected. "I had to know that you had the spiritual maturity to lead this team."

"I have to tell you, it made no sense to me at the time," Carl admitted. "I mean, I knew you wanted a person of faith to take this job, but I couldn't figure out why it was so important to you to understand where I was in my faith. I think I get it now."

"One last thing that's important for you to understand, Carl," Peter said, leaning forward to make it clear that this was an important point. "This approach calls all of us to a higher level of excellence in all we do, much higher than the old way of transactional fundraising. If we really expect to be used by God to help our supporters develop hearts that are rich toward God, we had better be doing our work at the highest level of professional excellence. God's work requires—*demands* actually—nothing less. It's important for you to hear that coming from the board."

Mike jumped in, "Carl, that was a realization that took me a while to understand. Stewards are actually called to a *higher* standard than owners, because of the nature of the true owner, God. That means that this approach had to be integrated throughout the entire organization. In development terms, that meant re-thinking our direct mail letters, acquisition strategy, even what we said at events and in our grant proposals. We are still asking questions and being challenged by the call to do all of our work with excellence."

Carl nodded slowly, indicating that he understood, but he would need to continue to process all of this, especially how it would impact the way he would lead.

A Glimpse
into the Kingdom

Driving away from the breakfast meeting, Walt gave Carl some time to let their conversation sink in. It was a critical moment in Carl's training. It had taken Walt, Mike, and Peter nearly five years to let this new, transformational approach to raising resources find its way into the fabric and culture of the entire ministry. They had several setbacks and lost some good development people during the process. Having won such a hard-fought and important battle, Walt was not about to take a step backward. His confidence in Carl was growing, but he knew that a lot of work was ahead if Carl was not only to embrace this approach himself but also to be the kind of leader needed to take Hands of Love into the future.

The two men were headed north, then east, toward a small town on the edge of the Mount Baker-Snoqualmie National Forest. They had a good two-hour drive ahead of them, so once they had settled into the HOV lanes on Interstate 5, Walt opened up the conversation again.

"So, how about that big question that I asked you to consider?"

"Oh yes, it almost got lost in all of the conversation this morning. Thanks for asking. In some way our discussion with Mike and Peter helped to answer it, but I would still like to hear more from you. Yesterday you made the comment that 'God is the fundraiser.' Can you help me understand what you meant by that?"

"Let me try," Walt replied. "You see the corn field over there? Well, a farmer went out one day and planted a bunch of seeds in the ground, covered them up, watered them, fertilized them, and did everything he could to help them grow. But at some point he had to just wait and hope and believe. A farmer can't *make* crops grow, and a faithful Christian fundraiser can't *make* people give, certainly not in a God-honoring way. That's *his* work. Part of my conversion came when I considered Paul's words to the Corinthians: that he can only plant, Apollos can only water, but it is God and God alone who brings the increase. I thought a lot about that in relationship to my work as a fundraiser. I realized that for my entire professional career, I had truly believed that not only was I expected to plant and water, but it was up to *me* to make the crop grow. Beyond that, I had to be sure that it was harvested, and that I was the only one doing the harvesting. I developed a scarcity mentality and believed that I needed to protect my ministry partners from other fundraisers. That's a huge burden to carry, being planter, waterer, grower, harvester, and defender."

"That pretty well sums up my career in fundraising," Carl replied. "I really didn't see any alternative, and my board held me accountable accordingly."

"Yup, that was my first ten years at Hands of Love as well. What a lousy way to make a living!"

"I guess I never thought of it that way," Carl replied thoughtfully. "I mean, I know our job carries a lot of stress, lots of pressure, but I just thought that was par for the course."

"Well, one day someone helped me understand that my job was not a harvester, or a grower—as if I could make that happen anyway—but as a faithful sower. Once I embraced the truth that God alone brings the increase, my whole approach to my work changed dramatically," Walt said with a deep sense of conviction.

"Let me ask you something, and I don't mean to be offensive," Carl said. "To some, that might seem like kind of a copout. I mean, did some people think that by saying that God is the fundraiser that you were kind of shirking your responsibilities and blaming any shortfall in income on God?"

Walt laughed. Then his tone turned serious.

"Oh yes, I lost a good friend and a pretty good fundraiser over that very issue. He just would not give up his control over the process. He insisted that what I was proposing was irresponsible," Walt said, shaking his head sadly. "A lot of people on our staff struggled with this idea. We'd all been taught, indoctrinated actually, with the idea that when it comes to fundraising, it was all up to us. The strange thing is, we always asked our ministry partners to pray about their decision. We just never allowed them the opportunity to do so. We were so clever and tenacious in our follow-up that we squeezed God out of the picture in order to be sure that we got what *we* wanted. I know that sounds pretty harsh, but when I look back on it, that's exactly what we did."

"No, actually it doesn't sound harsh at all," Carl replied. "It sounds like exactly the way I have worked my whole career. It's the only way, so you just do it and live with it. I have to tell you, Walt, there is some real freedom in knowing that there's a better way to do this, a real God-pleasing way."

Walt smiled broadly when Carl mentioned *freedom.*

"Freedom is a word that I have been careful not to overuse. I wanted to see if you would come to it on your own. But Carl, it's the single greatest word in this whole conversion process. It is freedom, absolutely! It's freedom for us, but it is also the greatest single blessing we offer our supporters. And it all starts with acknowledging that God is the fundraiser."

Carl just sat silently and nodded his head. Slowly, it was beginning to make sense to him.

Before long they began talking about their next appointment. Carl pulled out the file on Lela Ripley.

"So, tell me about Mrs. Ripley," he said.

"Well, there's a lot to tell, but it's really just better if you meet her yourself. I'll tell you this: you're about to meet a pretty remarkable woman. She may have more to do with my conversion than any other person. And the amazing thing is, she doesn't know it, not even to this day."

"You've never told her?" Carl asked in surprise.

"Nope. It just never seemed appropriate to tell her. I think when you meet her you'll understand why," Walt said.

Carl was intrigued by the mysterious nature of Walt's comments. It wasn't long before they pulled off the freeway and into a town that was a throwback to the early logging days in the Pacific Northwest. Time had certainly stood still there. Beautiful little tree-lined streets went off in two directions from the tiny downtown area that boasted two banks, a post office, and a neighborhood café. Walt drove down to the end of one of those streets and turned into the driveway of a small white home that seemed right out of an episode of *The Andy Griffith Show*.

The two men walked through the creaky gate of the white picket fence and made their way toward the front door. Before arriving at the door, Walt slipped off his wedding ring and a beautiful onyx ring that he wore on his right hand. He placed them both in his pants pocket and headed to the door.

Carl stopped him and asked, "What's with the rings?"

"You'll see," Walt replied.

Scarcely a minute after Walt rang the doorbell, the front door opened. There standing before them was Lela Ripley. She couldn't have been more than four feet ten inches tall and was so slight that it seemed a good gust of wind could send her flying up into the sky. Yet Carl could see that she was anything but frail.

Upon seeing Walt, she reached out her arthritic hands and grabbed his, holding them up in front of her as she spoke.

"Well, you are a sight for sore eyes. Thank you so much for coming to see me, Walt. You've made my day."

Walt smiled back at her and, for a moment, they just enjoyed being in each other's presence, standing face to face and holding each other's hands.

"Oh come now, let's get out of this chilly breeze," Lela said as she spun around and moved inside the house.

Walt and Carl followed, and as soon as they were inside the door she turned back and walked up to Carl, putting her two hands out. Carl realized this was her way of shaking hands. He put his two hands in hers and immediately understood why Walt had taken off his rings. For the next few moments, while still holding Carl's hands, Lela spoke to him, welcoming him into her home, thanking him for coming with Walt, and telling him how much Walt had meant to her over the years and how she looked forward to getting to know Carl as well. The more she spoke, the tighter she gripped his hands. He was amazed that this eighty-nine-year-old, tiny woman with significant arthritis had a grip that he swore could crush a walnut with ease. He could almost feel his rings cutting into the flesh of the adjoining fingers as Lela squeezed his hands more forcefully with every passing comment. He was about to reach the breaking point when she finally finished her welcome and let go.

Walt was doing all he could not to burst out laughing. The look on Carl's face was familiar to him. The first time Lela had held his hands like that it actually brought tears to his eyes. Since then, he had always slipped off his rings before his visit. He was sure that Carl would be doing the same from this point on. After she let go, Carl shot Walt a look that assured him of this.

"Now, come in and sit down and tell me what God has been doing in your life," she said as she worked her way through stacks of books and over to her favorite comfortable chair. Carl was amazed at the columns of books that surrounded her. He glanced at the titles and saw everything from the history of Islam to creation care to a biography on Winston Churchill and several books on science and religion. There were Bible commentaries, textbooks on economics, a beginners guide to astronomy, and three mystery novels.

"You must be a voracious reader, Mrs. Ripley," Carl said with admiration.

"My dear boy, we must exercise our brains and not let them get flabby. I may not be able to ski or hike like I used to, but the good Lord has blessed me with clear eyes even at eighty-nine, and so I use them to keep my brain fit.

"And please, call me Lela. I haven't been Mrs. Ripley since I stopped teaching eighth grade about twenty years ago. If you call me that again, I may ask you for your homework assignment," she said with a huge laugh.

"Lela, you're a delight. I just love coming here to visit you," Walt said, joining her in the laugh.

"Well, I do enjoy our visits Walt. That you would take the time to visit this crotchety old lady, well, it just blesses my soul," she replied. "I do have a bit of a bone to pick with you though."

Walt looked visibly concerned.

"Oh dear, please tell me what I've done."

Lela reached beside her chair and pulled out an envelope. It was clear that she had placed it there in preparation for this visit. She removed the envelope's contents with flair. She opened the paper, placed her reading glasses on her nose, and began to read aloud.

"Dear Mrs. Ripley, I cannot begin to thank you enough for

your generous gift to support our work in Guatemala. With this gift, we will be able to more than double the number of children whose lives will be…" she stopped and nodded her head, indicating that she was reading on silently to get to the part that she wanted to share. Then she continued. "I want you to know that we could not do this ministry without you, and it is because of the faithful and generous support of people like you that we are able to take the love of Christ to the people of Guatemala and around the world. Please accept my heartfelt thanks for this wonderful gift."

She sat the letter down on her lap, removed her reading glasses, and looked directly at Walt.

"Walt, this kind of thank you letter just will not do," she said while pointing her reading glasses at Walt, looking every bit the seasoned schoolteacher. "And you know exactly what I'm talking about."

Carl was taken aback by the whole scene. What possibly could have been wrong in the letter that caused such a strong reaction from this seemingly sweet little old lady? He didn't have to wait long for the answer.

Walt sat forward in his chair, shook his head apologetically, and replied, "I am so sorry, Lela. I usually catch those letters before they get sent to you. Please accept my apology," he said earnestly.

Carl still couldn't figure out what was going on.

Lela sat her glasses down, looking not the least bit satisfied.

"The point is not that I expect you to intercept these letters just *to me*. The question is why Hands of Love feels they need to send these letters in the first place. Why are you thanking and honoring people for doing the most basic act of obedience? You keep telling me that you want to help people understand that everything they have is the Lord's, but when they try to be faithful stewards, you thank them as if they had done some magnanimous act, as if this money was really theirs to do with as they pleased. You can't have it both ways, Walt. People will never learn to be stewards if they are constantly thanked like they are owners."

Carl was stunned. In all of his years of fundraising, he had never had a ministry partner scold him for *over*-thanking them. And this was no show—she was dead serious.

"I understand your concern, Lela. But not everyone, in fact precious few people, really understands what it is to be a faithful steward. We're trying to minister to our supporters to help them understand this, but were still at a place where most of them expect this kind of a thank you when they give. They would be as upset as you are if they *didn't* receive this letter."

Walt knew that this reply would not hold much water with Lela. Over the years, he had come to know her as a tenacious, no compromising steward. And she would not let him forget those times when he treated her as anything else.

"Carl, has Walt told you about the time that he came to ask me for a gift and told me the amount that he wanted me to give?" she asked, continuing to play the role of the stern schoolteacher.

Walt put his head in his hands and moaned.

Carl jumped at the chance to hear more about the transgressions of his mentor, and he sat forward in his chair with a look of great expectation.

"No, he didn't say word to me about it. But it sounds like

something I should know so that I can learn from it. Please, Lela, do tell me the story," Carl said while smiling from ear to ear.

Walt just continued to keep his face in his hands.

Lela pulled her chair around to face Carl so that he didn't miss a word.

"It was about three years ago—isn't that right, Walt?"

Walt spoke without taking his face out of his hands.

"Yes, I guess so, about three years ago."

"Yes, so three years ago Walt comes to visit, and he's excited about this new project they have going in Guatemala. I can hardly get him to sip on some lemonade or tell me the good things that God is doing in his life before he has a proposal out of his briefcase and shoved in front of me. He was very professional as always, but I could tell he was particularly agitated about this project. In fact, he was a lot more interested in this project than he was in finding out what God was doing in *my* life. A lot of pressure on him from the home office, I believe. Anyway, I chose to go along with it and listen to his 'pitch,' and he was quite convincing. He can be quite a charmer, you know," she said with a twinkle in her eye.

"I was pretty warm to the idea. I had two sisters and a nephew all spend time as missionaries in Guatemala, and I had traveled to the country six times on various church mission trips and one educational junket on behalf of our school district. So I was ready to take the proposal to the Lord in prayer and seek his guidance for how he would have me respond. Now Carl, I assume that you would not be working for Walt if you are not a man of God, am I correct?"

"Uh, yes absolutely," Carl replied as convincingly as he could.

"Well then, as a man of God, surely you believe that if every-thing we have belongs to him, then we should ask him about how we should invest it in his work, isn't that right?"

At this, Walt's head was out of his hands. He looked directly at Carl, for now the shoe was on the other foot. Carl knew what the right answer was, but he realized how much differently he would've answered this question just two days ago. So he was honest.

"I am beginning to understand that more and more every day, Lela."

"And that includes not only *where* we should invest his resources but *how much*, isn't that right, too?" she asked.

Carl had no doubt where this story was going. He had spent his fundraising career asking people to consider specific amounts to support the organizations he represented. He was about to learn how wrong he had been in doing so.

"Yes, I guess that makes sense," was the best reply he could muster. That would not do for Lela Ripley.

"Makes sense! It does far more than just makes sense, my dear boy. It is absolutely biblical. God's people must be invited to invest God's resources in God's work at the amount that God places on their heart. There is no room in this process for human guesswork. So imagine my surprise, my horror actually, when my dear friend Walt places in front of me a sheet of paper with my name on it that suggested that I contribute to this project with a gift in the amount that was stipulated in large bold print. Outra-geous! And this from a man of God!"

Clearly Lela was having great fun with this story. She

continued glancing over at Walt and smiling at his feigned agony as the story continued. She also smiled and winked at Carl, and he appreciated the fun, but he had no doubt there was a deep and profound sense of truth in what she was saying.

"Okay, enough, enough. My sins have been revealed, and I am truly repentant," Walt said, continuing the lighthearted nature of what they all knew was a very serious subject.

"Oh, but I am not finished," she continued. "Carl, I want you to know just how amazing our God is. After chastising Walt for such a blatant disregard for the work of the Holy Spirit in this process, I did promise him that I would pray about the opportunity. In the days that followed, I prayed many times over that piece of paper. I had crossed out that amount that had been 'suggested' for me, and I sought the Lord for guidance. After a few days, it was absolutely clear to me what I needed to do. Walt, would you like to finish the story?" she asked in a tone that let him know that it was not a request.

Walt seemed relieved to be able to bring the story to a conclusion.

"We received a lovely letter from Lela about a week after my visit informing us that she indeed would *not* be giving us the amount we requested, but an amount that the Lord had laid on her heart. We opened a check to find that it was four times the amount we asked for."

Lela leaned forward and spoke the concluding word.

"Never tell God what to do, and never tell God's people what they are to give. You just might end up underestimating the generosity of both."

All Carl could do was nod. This was another issue he was

going to need to chew on for quite a while, but when he looked into the eyes of this faithful servant of God, he had no answer to her challenge. Perhaps God really is the fundraiser.

"Well, that was fun," Walt said playfully. "And I thought you were my friend."

"Walt, I am more than your friend, I am your sister in Christ, and I love you dearly. If I didn't, I could never have had so much fun at your expense," she said, throwing her head back and enjoying another great laugh, which they all shared.

Carl and Walt spent two hours with Lela. Most of it was spent talking about what God was doing in each of their lives. Carl listened while Lela talked about her years in teaching, the loss of her dear husband fifteen years ago, and her four Bible studies that she leads in the community. Walt commented that he had never known a better Bible scholar than Lela, even though she only had a bachelor's degree in education she earned in 1944. It was when she spoke about her life as a steward that touched Carl the most. He had never heard anyone speak in such absolute terms about the faithfulness of God, the responsibilities of faithful stewardship, and the unmatchable joy of generous giving.

Toward the end of their conversation, Walt handed Lela two proposals that outlined some new work that was planned in Guatemala. She accepted them warmly and promised to pray for guidance over her reply.

"I don't know how much longer I'm going to be on this earth, but I want to be as faithful as I can to the very end. Once I'm gone to be with the Lord, you'll have no reason to drive all the way up here and waste away your afternoons," she said with a wink.

"Carl, you need to know that Lela has carefully planned for her estate after she is gone. Actually, Hands of Love owns this house, and she is living here under a retained life estate arrangement. She will indeed be faithful to the end," Walt said.

They all stood up, and Walt gave Lela a warm hug to signal their departure. Carl felt a strong need to let her know what this visit had done for him.

"Lela, I can't tell you how much it has meant to me to meet you. I'm kind of, well, on a journey of sorts. I'm trying to figure out this new way of fundraising—I mean, of raising up faithful stewards that Walt and the ministry have adopted. It's completely new and foreign to me. This visit has meant the world to me, and I just wanted you to know that."

She came over to Carl, took both of his hands, and spoke while looking directly into his eyes.

"I sense very strongly that you are God's man for this season at Hands of Love. But you will need to trust him like you have never trusted him before. Can you do that, Carl?"

Carl felt like he was about to answer God himself.

"I pray that I can, Lela, and I would be so grateful if you would pray for me that I can."

She smiled back at him and nodded her head.

"Indeed I will, Carl. Indeed I will."

THE BATTLE

W alt and Carl drove away from Lela's house enjoying a few minutes of silence just to let the experience sink in. Walt was pleased by Carl's first response.

"Imagine what we could do at Hands of Love if we had about a hundred Lela Ripleys."

"Well," Walt replied, "we have over a thousand people on our list of supporters, and a team of five stewardship officers…and a new director of stewardship."

Walt looked at Carl and smiled.

"So what you're saying," Carl replied thoughtfully, "is that I have just seen the reason I was hired. We need to help our people get to where Lela is as faithful, godly stewards."

"There and beyond. Lela would tell you that she still has a long way to go on her journey. But yes, she's a great example of a heart set free to be a joyous steward. She's not the only one among our supporters, but I wanted you to meet her early on to get a sense of how wonderful this job is when you get the chance to sit in the presence of someone whose heart is really rich toward God. I just love coming up here, although I never leave without something I need to chew on, and usually something I need to change. But I guess that's part of the fun."

"So, I'm still processing this idea of leaving the amount of the ask up to the discretion of our ministry supporters…and God, of course. Is there *ever* a time when you ask for a specific amount?" Carl asked a little hesitantly.

"Sure. The key, Carl, is to listen as intently as we can to the leading of the Holy Spirit. Usually for me that means an invitation to support programs and projects with gifts that can come in a range of sizes, but every once in awhile I have felt led to invite someone to give specifically for a project or program at a set amount. Sometimes I have sensed God's leading not to make an invitation at all."

"Wow! That takes a lot of prayer and discernment. That's the scary part for me. I'm not a spiritual giant. What if I don't hear right?"

"Well, I have found that if we are open and willing, God is faithful. It has helped me to remember Ephesians chapter six, where we are told to pray in the Spirit on all occasions with all kinds of prayers and requests."

"I can do that," Carl replied.

"I think that's all God asks," Walt added.

They had reached the interstate and began driving south back toward Seattle for their final appointment of the day. Walt had carefully chosen these two visits for Carl's second day, although he felt he was taking a risk in ending his training time with a visit to Andrew Brady. Walt would need to prepare Carl for this visit, but Carl had other things on his mind.

"Walt, something has been troubling me since our conversation this morning with Mike and Peter, and I think I feel it even more acutely now, after our time with Lela. Do we have time to talk about it?"

"Absolutely, but I do want to leave some time to prepare you for our final visit. So shoot."

"Peter told me that the board would hold me responsible for the spiritual leadership of my team. That seemed to be as much if not more important to him and Mike than anything else we talked about. I'm not sure I know exactly what that will require, or, frankly, if I'm up to it. I mean, I have a strong personal spiritual life, but I would not consider myself a spiritual leader, not at all. I'm not really sure just *what* it is that I'm supposed to be leading them *to*. That's not very articulate, but can you give me some help here?"

"Let me give it a try and see if you find this helpful," Walt replied.

They slipped into the familiar HOV lanes on the freeway. Walt put his Prius on cruise control.

"The first thing that I would say, Carl, is that we all need to understand and embrace the idea that this work that we are doing is ministry, *real* ministry. All of my career, I was taught to believe that fundraising was the 'necessary evil' that someone had to do in order to secure the money that was needed for real ministry to happen. I can remember colleagues being surprised when I attended chapel or offered to lead prayer at staff meetings. They just didn't equate fundraising with anything remotely spiritual. I'm not sure some of them even believed I needed to be a Christian in order to do my job. It's amazing how much we've allowed this split between the work of raising funds and the work that the funds make happen. All that changed when I realized that the work we were doing was ministry work. But it goes way beyond that. Not only is our work ministry, but I am coming to believe that it may be among the most difficult and challenging, and, therefore, among the most important ministry that's being done anywhere. You remember earlier we talked about freedom, and you used the word to describe what it means when someone becomes a real steward?"

"Yep, and that was a real paradigm shift for me," Carl said with a nod.

"It is for all of us. We've talked about the fact that our primary job in raising funds for Christian work is to be used by God to help set people free, and sometimes they help *us*," Walt said, shaking his head while thinking of the conversation with Lela. "That's a pretty remarkable ministry. And it seems to me that we have a real challenging call given that most of the churches I've attended don't do a great job of talking about money or helping people become one-kingdom, joyful stewards. Sometimes I feel like we're out there on our own in this battle."

"Battle? That seems like a pretty hard term. Do you really mean it that way?" Carl asked.

"Absolutely. I believe that doing our work faithfully puts us in the greatest battle of our lives. Think about it for a minute. Where else in our world does the enemy have as great a control than in issues about money? The church doesn't like to talk about it, and people don't like to hear about it, so we end up pretty ignorant about what the Bible really has to say about it. That's what I see all the time: good, godly people who want to live their lives for Christ but have no clue as to what the Bible says about their money and possessions. So they give God the spiritual part of their lives but continue to be their own lord over everything else.

"Back to the two kingdoms," Carl replied.

"Exactly. Now you and I come along as Christian development professionals and ask them to pray over their decisions when they're living in that old, two-kingdom mindset. And all the time the enemy is telling them 'that's okay, because if the Bible had more to say about money, surely the church would be teaching it.' So we go in battling misperception, misinformation, and general ignorance about what it means to be a godly steward. And beyond that, we have an enemy who works desperately to keep people in bondage. He has our consumer culture, pride, and lack of biblical literacy all on his side. Those are pretty powerful weapons to confront. So yes, without any doubt, I see this as a major spiritual battle."

Walt gave Carl a moment to process.

"Now I feel even less equipped not only to do this job but to lead others," Carl said shaking his head. "That's a huge expectation for anyone."

"But Carl, this is not our battle. It belongs to the Lord. That's the only hope we have, but it is a huge hope! And that's why it's absolutely critical we be spiritually prepared for this work. That's what Peter was talking about. It's not about our strength or even leading by our own efforts, but allowing God through the Holy Spirit to prepare us and equip us and empower us for this work. It's all about submission to his direction. Do you see that?"

Carl drew a long sigh. He thought for a few moments before responding. Then he said carefully, "I can see it in my mind, but my heart is still uncertain, and now my stomach hurts."

They both laughed as Walt moved them back into traffic and prepared to take the next exit.

"Your staff won't expect you to be a spiritual giant or an accomplished Bible teacher. They just want you to be genuine, to be as passionate as they are about spiritual preparation, and to hold them accountable, as they will you."

"But I'm just not sure *how* I am supposed to help them be prepared. I mean, what does it look like? What's involved, and how do I know that I'm doing it well?"

"One way is to follow a set of values that we all agreed to a number of years ago. We have them written down and refer to them on a weekly basis. It's basically a set of commitments that we have made to each other and to our work. If you do nothing more than keep those in front of everyone and hold them accountable for how they work to achieve them, that'll be a major step in the right direction."

Carl was relieved to know that there was something written down that he could follow, and he was anxious to learn more about this set of commitments. The thought flashed in his head as to whether or not he could embrace them all himself.

He sat silently and shook his head as he began to consider the full weight of these last two days and all that it would mean not only for his leadership at Hands of Love but also for his own life as a husband, father, and follower of Jesus. This was all so far from what he had expected when he took the job, but the quiet process of conversion was already well underway in his spirit, and he had reached the point where he never wanted to go back. He was in, for whatever that meant, and all he could do was hold on for what he was beginning to realize would be the ride of his life.

ON HIS OWN

A s they pulled onto Pacific Highway, Carl opened the
manila file on Andrew Brady and began to read. It was a
profile of a longtime faithful supporter of the ministry with gifts
that ranged from two thousand to twenty-five thousand dollars.
The notes on Andrew were substantial, and Carl could tell that
he and Walt had spent a lot of time together over the years. Carl
assumed that this was another Lela Ripley kind of visit, so after
glancing at the background information, he placed the file back
in his briefcase and commented to Walt.

"Mr. Brady looks like a solid supporter. Anything I should
know before we get there?"

"Oh yes, plenty," Walt replied in a serious tone that surprised
Carl.

"Okay, I'm all ears," Carl replied.

"Carl, I've taken a bit of a chance by setting our last appointment with Andrew. On paper I know he looks like your rather
standard, faithful supporter. In a lot of ways he is. I have never

visited him where he didn't follow up with a gift. He always gives when asked, and he really loves what we do. That's the easy part. The challenge," Walt said shaking his head, "the challenge is that this man has never known one ounce of joy in any gift he's given. I've never met a man more in bondage to fear and anxiety over, well, about everything in his life. He was divorced about ten years ago and has never had a very good relationship with either of his kids. And you want to know the funny part? He owns a toy store!"

"I saw that in his file," Carl replied. "He owns Toys on Parade down on Market Street. That's a huge store. We just discovered it, and my kids love it in there. I guess it is somewhat ironic that the guy who owns a toy store can be so sad."

"Well, that's Andrew. Every time we visit, I try to help him connect with the joy of giving, but I must say I don't think I've gotten very far after all these years. I've even told him my favorite story about the joy of giving, a story about my grandson."

"I'd love to hear that story," Carl said. "Do we have time?"

"I think so," Walt replied. "It's one I tell whenever I can. I was playing with my then two-year old grandson in his yard, where he collected some white quartz-like stones that he liked. Before going into the house for a snack, he packed a few of them in the pocket of his jeans. We washed up, and he sat at the table for his favorite snack, a piece of string cheese. When I looked in my daughter's refrigerator, there was only one piece left. I gave it to him and sat down across from him. He was concerned that I didn't have one. He didn't want to eat his because I didn't have one. Pretty soon, he twisted and twisted to break it and give me half. It was quite mangled, but I was touched that he wanted me to have it. A little later, he rediscovered his rocks in his pocket. He pulled them out and examined them. One in particular had shiny silver streaks on it. That was his best rock, and after examining it carefully, he decided he wanted me to have it. 'You can have my best rock, Grandpa,' he said, throwing his arms around my neck."

Walt paused as a little emotion welled up inside him. He took a deep breath and continued.

"I reflected later as to how a two-year old learns to give half his snack or his very best rock to someone he loves. I came to the conclusion that he is hard-wired that way. He is made in the image of God. It is the nature of God to give: God so loved the world that he *gave*…. God's love is demonstrated in the act of giving."

They pulled to a stoplight. Walt turned to look directly at Carl.

"Carl, we need to come to the place where we see the act of giving directly to God as more important than even the act of giving to God's work or the ministry. Giving to God produces great joy, just like my grandson felt when he gave his best rock to someone he loves deeply. It is interesting that I was touched watching him tear half that cheese to give to me. *I gave it to him in the first place.* I owned it first and gave it to him, but I was still pleased when he gave half of it back. That is joyful giving."

Carl was moved by Walt's story. He was turning the scene over in his mind when Walt suddenly shifted back to the discussion about the meeting with Andrew.

"The thing about Andrew is that he really loves Jesus, but I'm not sure he has ever understood just how much Jesus loves *him*. So he goes through life fearful and anxious about every-thing. I almost hate to ask him for support. I know he feels good about supporting us, but I also know he worries desperately over money. I can imagine the kind of anxiety he feels after he writes us a check. As I said, I've tried everything I can think of, and I don't think I've made much progress with Andrew. So—" Walt paused for a long moment as if he wasn't really sure how to fin-ish the thought, "—I thought I would give *you* a try."

The comment shot through Carl like an electric shock.

"*Me?* What do you mean, Walt? You want *me* to talk to him about joyful giving?"

"Well, I can't think of a better way for you to make the tran-sition from training to execution than having a go with Andrew," Walt replied with a sly grin on his face.

"We'll make this a normal visit," he continued, "but I would like you to feel free to speak your heart. I think Andrew needs to hear a different voice than mine. Are you okay with that?"

Carl thought for a moment as Walt pulled the car to a stop outside of a suburban home in North Seattle. *Why not?* he thought. *I'll need to do this sooner or later anyway, and it might as well be while Walt is with me.*

"I'll do my best, Walt, but don't expect too much," Carl replied.

It wasn't long before the two men were at the door and invited into a spacious home with a breathtaking view of Mount Rainier. Andrew Brady was in his early sixties. His full head of white hair was combed back in a style that gave him every bit the look of a stately Scotsman. His home was filled with pic-tures, souvenirs, and artifacts from Scotland, interspersed with a curious collection of antique toys. *Quite an eclectic décor*, Carl thought.

There was only a small amount of polite conversation before Andrew's comments about work proved Walt's perception to be correct.

"Sure, we've had a pretty positive year, but that says nothing about what might be ahead. I remember back in eighty-five when we broke all of our sales records—two years later we were struggling to keep the doors open. You don't forget those kinds of things. Not if you're smart. I'm probably as well off financially right now as I have been in a long time, but I've never felt more strongly about the need to hold onto it given these strange political times. You just never know what the government's going to do next to try to pick your pocket. I wish I had better news, but tell me, what's going on at Hands of Love?"

Walt smiled. He had heard this a dozen times before. Andrew always had a reason why this was not a good time to be asking him for money. Walt marveled over the years at how many reasons he could come up with despite a growing business that kept him financially well off.

"I can understand your concern, Andrew, but it seems to me the good Lord has always been there for you, and it's pretty certain he always will be. Don't you agree?" Walt asked carefully.

"Of course he will," Andrew shot back a little pointedly. "But that gives us no cause to test him. The Lord looks out for those who look out for themselves. Just because he's blessed me doesn't mean I can be foolhardy with what I have. Remember, it was the *wise* steward who was welcomed into the kingdom by his master."

Walt accepted the comments, even though he questioned Andrew's application of scripture. He shot a quick look over to Carl, letting him know that he was looking for his input.

"Yes, I get your point Andrew. I'm just saying that we should be able to live our lives with a sense of peace about God's promise and provision. While we are wise stewards of what we are given, we're also commanded to not be anxious for what lies ahead. I know that's tough to balance, but I think that's where God wants us. Don't you?" Walt asked with a little hesitancy.

Andrew considered the comment and decided not to go any further down this particular line of discussion. He was curious about Carl, and so he turned his attention to him and asked, "so, what has this old veteran been teaching you?"

Carl smiled back at Andrew and drew a deep breath, shooting off a silent prayer for help as he formulated his reply.

"Well, I must say it's been a pretty amazing two days," Carl admitted.

"Really? How do you mean that?" Andrew asked.

"Well, for one, I never realized how important it was for me to be a generous giver in order to be effective at my work of inviting others to give. I think more than anything, Walt has challenged me to think about my own attitudes toward giving and how they will affect my work."

"He'll certainly do that," Andrew said emphatically, smiling back at Walt. Carl decided to continue his thoughts.

"You know, I've been doing what I call major gifts fundraising for a long time, but I've never been a really joyful giver myself. It never seemed to be an issue before. Walt and I both hope that you would be blessed by the way you are asked and by what you choose to give—that your gift would be both generous and joyful. But I can't sit here with any credibility and be a part of this process unless *I'm* a generous and joyful giver in my own life. So I have to be honest with you and say that I'm struggling a little here. I guess I have a long way to go on this journey, and I probably have little right to sit here and ask you for a major gift."

Carl was surprised at his own words and hopeful that he had not stepped over the line.

"Wow! I guess that's about as honest as I can be," he added.

There was silence for a few moments.

Suddenly, Andrew stood up and walked over to a desk where he picked up a pipe, tapped some new tobacco in the bowl, put it to his lips, and lit the sweet smelling tobacco. He soon began emitting large puffs of smoke into the room. He turned back, sat down, and stared back at his two guests.

"So what are you going to do then?" he asked to Carl's surprise.

Carl struggled for a moment to consider a response, but Andrew continued before he could say anything.

"You came all this way to talk to me about giving. How do you intend for us to spend our time if you're not in a position to ask me?" Andrew asked.

Carl was not sure what came over him, but the answer jumped into his head with amazing clarity. He turned to Andrew and smiled.

"I guess I'm going to ask you to join me on the journey," Carl replied warmly. "I can't tell you that I'm any further along than you are. In fact, I'm probably way behind. But I'm convinced that God is calling me to be a more faithful steward. For me, that means giving up the little kingdom that I've built for myself and turning everything over to him. It means trusting him more than I've ever trusted him before. And I hope and believe that means being able to give more freely, more joyously, and more generously than I ever have in my life. My wife and I have a lot of work to do, but I can tell you we're both committed to this journey. So, all I can really do is ask if I can journey with you?"

Walt looked over at his new hire. For the first time since he had offered Carl the position, he knew with certainty he had made the right decision. He shot a silent prayer of thanks to God and then waited to hear Andrew's response.

Andrew worked his pipe like an old pro, keeping the tobacco embers glowing and gracefully blowing circles of smoke out around the edges of his mouth. He studied Carl carefully as he chewed on the stem of his pipe, aware that both men were waiting for his response. He shifted in his chair and looked up to the ceiling, deep in thought. Then his gaze came back down and fixed on Carl.

"It's not my choosing, you know. Worrying that is. My father lived through the depression and he drove into us that having money meant independence, control, and the assurance that your family would never starve. The greatest accomplishment a man could achieve in my father's eyes was absolute independence, never having to rely on anyone for anything…*ever*," Andrew said with a bite of anger in his tone. "So that's how I lived my life. I understand what the Good Book says about being generous. I also know how quickly money can be made and lost. I'd just like someone to help me understand how to hold those two things together. Can you help me do that?"

Carl was amazed at the comment. This was his moment to put into practice all that he'd been learning. He smiled and slowly nodded his head.

"I can only promise to go down the road with you and see where God will lead us. I have a lot to learn, Andrew, so I can't make any guarantees. But I would sure enjoy the opportunity to meet with you and talk this through together."

"I'd like that," Andrew replied. "This guy's been working on me for a long time, and I appreciate him more than I probably ever let him know. So maybe I'm ready to think about this a little more than I have in the past. Come back and see me on a Thursday afternoon. That's when I have some time away from the store. We'll see where it goes."

For the remainder of their time, the three of them talked about projects at Hands of Love. Carl and Walt left Andrew two proposals to consider with prayer, and Andrew and Carl set their next appointment for an upcoming Thursday afternoon.

When Walt and Carl were back into the car and on their way, Carl waited for Walt to comment. Once he could shift his focus away from navigating the busy traffic of a late afternoon Seattle commute, he spoke.

"That was pretty remarkable, Carl. I can't believe the progress you've made in such a short time."

Carl replied, "I'm not sure I did much but just admit how little progress I've made. I really don't feel equipped to help Andrew understand much of anything at all, but somehow I feel like we can figure it out together."

"So, would you say that Andrew needs you in order to carry out his calling to be a faithful steward?"

"Yes, I guess that's one way to put it."

"And what about the Ortlunds?" Walt asked.

Carl wasn't sure where this was going, but as he thought about it, he had to agree.

"I can see how you could say that they need us to move further along on their journey as well."

"Carl, I want to share something with you that only makes sense once you have come a long ways down this process of conversion. To most everyone stuck in the old way of thinking about fundraising, this would sound, well, pretty absurd, I guess. But I think it is the core of what we have been discussing these past few days."

Carl was definitely intrigued. Walt continued.

"The conventional wisdom is that ministries need their supporters in order to operate, to exist. We go at our work with this 'needy' mindset and treat our supporters as if they only have things to give and we have all of the need. But from a biblical steward's perspective, the truth is actually the opposite. As God's people, we are given the privilege and calling to be faithful and wise stewards of what God has given to us. But to do that, we need credible places to give to, ways to invest God's resources that are both efficient in using money and effective in employing it for kingdom purposes. Without well-run organizations and ministries, it is very hard to be a faithful steward of our funds. And we need people to encourage us in our journey as stewards. When we do our job well, we provide the place and means for God's people to carry out their calling, to be obedient and faithful in an effective way. And we meet a need they have for someone to walk with them in this stewardship journey. So in truth, our supporters need *us* and the ministries we represent. That's why this is ministry and not fundraising."

Carl nodded slowly as he thought through Walt's comments. He was surprised at how sensible it all sounded, and how ridiculous it would have seemed to him just two days ago.

"I think I get it, Walt. Although it is a pretty amazing way to think about our work. It really turns everything on its head. But that's what I felt when I was talking to Andrew, like I hade something he needed, which was far more important than what I thought I needed from him."

"So your time with him is a ministry investment."

"Yes, I guess so. And I'm looking forward to helping him more, but it's going to take some time. I'm not sure I can do this with every ministry partner."

"That's one of those commitments I was telling you about," Walt replied, "being willing to invest the time in building kingdom relationships. There are no shortcuts, not if we believe this is ministry. And what you are going to be doing with Andrew, what you've already done, is definitely ministry."

"So, how many are there?" Carl asked.

"How many commitments? We have seven. I have them on a laminated card that I carry with me. There should be one in the glove box."

Carl pulled it out and examined it as Walt continued speaking.

"I can give them to you in a nutshell."

As he did, Carl followed along on the card.

1. *Be spiritually prepared for the battle.*
2. *Trust God to be the fundraiser.*
3. *Don't make decisions without prayerful discernment.*
4. *Be willing to invest the time in building kingdom relationships.*
5. *Always make the ministry more important than the money.*
6. *See and value accountability.*
7. *Be sure God gets the glory.*

"Everyone has these written down and agrees to them?" Carl asked.

"Yup, it's a requirement to work in the development department at Hands of Love."

"So, how come you hired me without ever mentioning them?" Carl asked.

"I was concerned that you would say you agree to them without really understanding what they meant and what it would require of you. I figured after these two days together, you'd either be ready to embrace them or we'd be going a different direction."

"So this really was a test?" Carl asked with some surprise.

"Yes, I have to admit it was. I had such a strong sense that you were the right person for this job when I hired you, but I left open the possibility that I'd made a mistake. I'm glad to say my original instinct was right," Walt said with a warm smile.

"So what do you think of the commitments?" he continued.

"There's a lot there to think through, but they all sound like steps in the journey," Carl replied.

The two days ended for Walt and Carl where it had begun, back at the headquarters of HOLI. The two men stood silently in the parking lot looking at the front entrance. This was a moment of transition, and neither spoke for a moment.

Walt broke the silence.

"Well, that's the end of our official training. Why don't you head home and have a nice evening with Cheryl? We'll pick it up in the morning with the staff meeting."

Carl was appreciative of an early departure and a chance to talk all of this through with Cheryl. He was anxious to tell her about Lela and the breakthrough with Andrew. He also wanted to continue their conversation from the night before. He was realizing just how critical it was for the two of them to make some serious decisions regarding their own attitude toward giving.

Carl nodded and smiled at Walt.

"I can't thank you enough for these past two days, Walt. Thanks for your patience with me and your confidence in me. I'm not sure I would have had the same if I were in your shoes."

"Sure you would! I think you can spot talent and heart as well as I can. And you'll need to as you build our team here. But it *has* been a great two days, Carl. You're going to do well."

As Carl prepared to shake Walt's hand, Walt turned away and fished through his briefcase. To Carl's surprise, he produced a long, thin, gift-wrapped box and handed it to him.

"What's this?" Carl asked.

"Just open it," Walt replied.

Carl sat his briefcase down and tore through the wrapping at one end of the box. He slid out a mahogany desk plaque with a brass plate. He turned it so he could read it in the fading evening light.

> *"There are three conversions necessary to every man; the head, the heart and the purse."*
> *– Martin Luther*

Carl smiled broadly and looked at Walt, nodding his head. "Amen. Thanks, Walt."

"I have had that saying on my desk for the past ten years. It reminds me of the battle we're in and the ministry we have," Walt replied. "I hope it'll do the same for you."

Carl let those be the last words spoken between them on these two momentous days. He shook Walt's hand and stood and watched as his mentor walked through the doors of Hands of Love and disappeared into the glow of the lobby lights.

Carl looked down again at the plaque and rubbed his finger across the engraved words, reading them again.

"The third conversion is the hardest, I think. God help me," he said quietly.

He pushed the plaque back into its box and placed it in his briefcase as he turned and walked to his car. He wondered just what tomorrow would bring. He would be stepping into his role as Director of Stewardship, beginning with an all-staff meeting. Every eye would be on him to see what his two days with Walt had produced.

Never in his life had he needed to rely so completely on the presence and power of God than he would have to tomorrow. And somehow, after his two days with Walt, that seemed like exactly the right place for his heart to be.

EPILOGUE

C arl peered through the slats of his office window blinds at the nervous new recruit sitting in the waiting room at Hands of Love. He drew a deep sigh as he considered the work he had ahead of him. It had been ten years since those first two days on the road with Walt. Since then the stewardship staff at the ministry had grown to nine full-time people, and it was getting harder to find experienced development professionals who understood their work as a ministry calling. For the first time, Carl had decided to hire someone from a secular fundraising background in the hope that they would make the conversion he had been going through since coming to HOLI. He smiled when he considered just how much the guy looked like him when he first met Walt.

Walt had been retired now for seven years. He came by from time to time to maintain the relationships that were so important to him. Scarcely had a week gone by in the past ten years that Carl didn't think back on some moment during those two days together with Walt. The conversion that began during those five visits set Carl, and Cheryl, on an amazing journey. They had sold their house and moved into a much smaller place so they could free up additional money to invest in God's work. They had learned to pray over decisions. They studied scripture together, and they found friends who were committed to the same stewardship goals. In all, they slowly began to discover the joy of giving, the reward of a heart that is rich toward God. Their simple lifestyle and generous spirit were a shining witness to friends and family, but Cheryl would tell you that she and Carl received more than what they ever gave away.

Carl looked at the screen on his new laptop and reviewed the files on the people that he and his new employee would be visiting. He smiled when he saw the name Andrew Brady. After Lela Ripley had passed away, Andrew had become Carl's new best example of a joyful, godly steward. Through months of discussions and prayer, they had, together found their way down the road of becoming faithful stewards.

The Ortlunds were also on the list. The week following his days with Walt, Carl asked if HOLI would write a refund check for the thousand dollar gift given by the Ortlunds in response to his ill-timed ask. He scheduled a very reluctantly agreed-to visit and presented them the check, an apology, and an explanation of all that he had learned from Walt. It still took several visits over more than two years to gain their full trust, but with a loving spirit and consistency, Carl had won them over, and now they were one of many couples that had journeyed with Carl and Cheryl into joyful giving.

Carl would have taken his new recruit to visit Jack Meacham, but he was with Mike on his seventh trip overseas to visit the projects he was supporting. In the past year, Jerry Shepherd, the ministry partner Carl fondly remembered visiting on his first day with Walt, had joined the board, which Peter still chaired.

As Carl pondered the names and stories that filled his laptop screen, he realized that even though he had faced his demons, he still struggled with the temptation to shortcut the process on visits and focus on the gift instead of the giver. Now he mostly won that battle, but he was constantly amazed at how often and how vigorously he continued to have to fight it.

Carl collected his things and placed them in his briefcase. The last item was a narrow, gift-wrapped box. He picked it up and played with it between his fingers before placing it deep within the inner pocket of his coat. He reached down and picked up the plaque from his desk and read the words again. As he did, a knock came at his door. His new team member was waiting, anxious to begin his first day, having no idea what challenges lay ahead of him.

Carl drew a deep breath as he placed the plaque back on his desk. He grabbed his briefcase and walked to the door to answer it, but he stopped short before reaching for the handle. He thought about how Walt must have felt those ten long years ago, and as he did, he prayed quietly, "God, help me help this young man down this road. Open his heart to this journey. Help him to embrace this third conversion. And dear Lord, set him free."

A PERSONAL WORD
TO MINISTRY SUPPORTERS

I wrote about Lela, Andrew, the Ortlunds, and Jack with you in mind. I pray that somewhere in their stories you have found yourself. Perhaps you related with Lela's faithfulness in prayer and trust in the Spirit, or maybe with Andrew's lack of joy in giving and his constant worrying about his money. You may have resonated with Steve and Kathy's frustration over "fundraisers" who seem only interested in your money, or perhaps with the guilt that motivated Jack in his decisions to support God's work.

What we all have in common is the journey we travel on to becoming the joyful, obedient, and faithful stewards God created us to be. I hope that you will consider carefully where you are on that journey. Look back to where you have been, what victories you have achieved, and what lessons you have learned. Look ahead to where God might be leading you. And look squarely at where you are today. As you do, let me ask you how you would answer Walt's questions. Where have you experienced your greatest joy in giving? Do you associate giving with great joy?

Regardless of where you are today, there is one thing of which I am certain: God is calling you to go further down the road. He is calling you into a deeper relationship with him. He is calling you to trust him more deeply, to follow him more closely, and to lose your life to him more completely.

The evidence of our continued journey down this road is a growing sense of real freedom. It is perhaps God's greatest gift to us. When we allow Christ to be Lord of every area of our lives, we are set free to live for him. When we set aside our ownership ways and joyfully take on the mantel of the faithful steward, we are set free to be used by God in mighty ways. When we open ourselves up for the work of the Spirit within us, the work of cultivating a heart that is rich toward God, we are set free to know the joy of being faithful stewards.

The great question of our day is simply this: Do you want to be set free? Christ is standing down the road, calling you to join him on the journey of a lifetime. It is the journey you were created to take. It is your joy and your destiny as a child of the King. Won't you set aside all of the seemingly important things that encumber you, all the temptations to personal kingdom building that vie for your attention, and all of the empty promises of this world that offer happiness but steal real joy?

Jesus is waiting for you, for every one of us. He is calling to us, reaching out for us, and offering to us a true life—the life of the faithful steward, the joyful giver, the heart that is set free. And it is sealed with the promise that "if Christ sets you free, you will be free indeed."

Welcome to the journey!

A Personal Word
to Christian Development
Professionals

I wrote about Carl and Walt with you in mind. I pray that you found yourself somewhere in this story. For some of you, this may be a confirmation and reminder of something you have believed for years. For others, this may be as revolutionary to you as it was to Carl.

I wrote this story because I am convinced that our work is radically different from a secular approach to fundraising. I wrote it to encourage those who understand this and struggle to live it out everyday. I wrote it to challenge those who remain stuck in old fundraising paradigms but who long to be set free. And, frankly, I wrote it to upset those who remain unconvinced and believe that our work really is the necessary evil that must be done to raise the money so that so-called real ministry can take place.

If you embrace this approach but struggle to live it out as faithfully as you would like, be encouraged. You are on a great journey that will have its peaks and valleys, but God is faithful. Re-read the seven commitments and carry the card with you.

Gather like-minded colleagues around you for prayer, support, and accountability. And start each day with the joyful thought that you are called to be used by God to set people free. How cool is that?

If you are just now beginning to embrace this new paradigm, then I challenge you to pray for boldness and an uncompromising spirit as you break free from the bondage of the old ways of fundraising that you are so accustomed to doing. Let me warn you, this conversion can't easily be made slowly and incrementally. It requires a wholesale *metanoia* (change resulting from a conversion) that is as radical as the end result it seeks to attain. Breaking bondages is not a methodical process, it is a revolution of the spirit that produces an uncompromising and resolute commitment to see everything we do in light of the call to minister to our supporters, raise up godly stewards, and be used by God to set people free. Most importantly, it will begin by working in you that same freedom and joy.

Finally, if you are among those who refuse to accept this teaching but insist on hanging onto practices and techniques that produce transactions without transformation, then I pray you will be upset and unnerved by this book. I pray that Carl and Walt's stories will stay with you and be used by God to slowly open your heart and mind to these important truths.

Ours is a high and holy calling for all who are willing to examine their own hearts first and then step into the battle of their lives. It is more than raising money for God's work—it *is* God's work. It *is* ministry. It is answering the call to make disciples whose hearts are rich toward God. It is the offer of freedom to a world in bondage, and for that reason it is a profession of generosity, of hope, and of great joy. May God bless you as you are used by him to be a blessing to everyone you serve.

A Personal Word
to Ministry Leaders
and Board Members

I wrote about Walt, Carl, Peter, and Mike with you in mind. As you heard from Peter and Mike, no development team can be fully successful in making the third conversion without the uncompromising support of the CEO and board of the ministries and organizations they serve. This conversion is both personal and communal. It starts in the heart of every Christian as God calls them on their journey of faith and obedience. But it does not stop there. The conversion makes its way into the life of the community of God's people. As it does, it affects systems, policies, and cultures.

I believe one of the greatest gifts any ministry leader can give to his or her organization is the cultivation of a culture of giving. Such a culture is constantly experiencing this conversion and engendering in its people the values of God's kingdom with regard to our call to be faithful stewards. When a community begins to embrace this conversion, when God sets communities of people free, they become a powerful force for the work of the kingdom.

What are you doing to help your development team make this conversion? How does your board support them and join them in this effort? How is their work communicated to the rest of the organization?

Organizations as well as individuals are embarked on a journey of faith and faithfulness. For an organization, this journey is influenced primarily by its culture. And ministry leaders are culture keepers. They are tasked to define reality, articulate values, and exhibit consistent behaviors that become the cultural moorings of the organization. When organizations define their reality in kingdom terms, articulate their values in alignment with biblical, holistic stewardship, and exhibit behaviors that indicate their commitment to the journey of the faithful steward, they engender a culture of giving.

Board members, are you committed personally to this journey for yourselves, seeking to be faithful stewards whose hearts are rich toward God? You are the model for your communities. Generosity in giving to your organization starts with you. Others will support your work as they see you giving generously and joyfully.

Ministry leaders, are you willing to start the entire process of building a culture of generosity by looking internally at your own attitudes and actions? Are you willing to lead by example, not as a perfect giver but as a co-journeyer on the path to becoming a more faithful steward? And will you call you organization to do the same, supporting your development team in their process of entering the battle and being used by God to set people free?

This is a bad time to get good at doing old things. The new wine of this biblical way of raising ministry resources requires new wineskins. May God bless you as you lead your organizations in building those new wineskins through the cultivation of a culture of generous, joyful giving that reflects the image of our God who "so loved the world that he gave..."